CW01648486

I do believe that you are two of the gamest ladies in the world," said Bob admiringly, "and I am going to have you made members of this club right here and now!" He raised his hand for silence and explained to the amazed members how he had conspired to have us enter the hall that night.

"And now," he said in conclusion, "these two ladies wish to become members of our club, and I do not think that there will be any objections to admitting them to our secrets."

"No, no," shouted the men, "let them in! Let them in!" And we were welcomed by all of them.

"Shall we initiate them?" one asked, and they all agreed that since we had gone through it, we should be initiated like the rest. At this part of my story I have an impulse to hide part of the happenings, but having promised to tell all of it, I will go ahead and do so.

Also by PAUL LITTLE:

Dangerous Lessons
The Lustful Turk
The Delicious Daughter
Tears of the Inquisition
Double Novel
Chinese Justice
The Discipline of Odette
All the Way
Slaves of Cameroon
The Prisoner
Autobiography of A Flea III
End of Innocence
Captive Maidens
Slave Island
Red Dog Saloon
Passion in Rio
Lust of the Cossacks
Turkish Delights
Poor Darlings

TUTORED IN LUST

Paul Little

MASQUERADE BOOKS, INC.
801 SECOND AVENUE
NEW YORK, N.Y. 10017

Tutored in Lust

First Masquerade Edition 1991

Second printing September 1994

ISBN 1-878320-78-5

Cover photograph by Robert Chouraqui

Cover design by Julie Miller

Manufactured in the United States of America
Published by Masquerade Books, Inc.
801 Second Avenue
New York, N.Y. 10017

CHAPTER ONE

I

I have been advised in writing this story of my life not to use my own name, as it would not only give me away, but too easily give away the personalities and the doings of others. So, with your kind permission, I will provide the parties concerned with names that are entirely different from their real cognomina.

However, I assure you that this is the only part of my story that has been changed. From beginning to end, all else in this strange narrative is the truth and nothing but.

My motive in writing is twofold. First, I have been assured that this story is going to mean a lot of money to me. Second, foolish as it may seem, I have been dared to write the story of my life. The dare is possibly the main reason for my efforts, because I have never been known to refuse a dare in my life.

Now, of course, I must first tell you a bit about myself and my circumstances. My name, for the purpose of this narrative at least, is Michelle. My intimate friends also call me Mike, a diminutive not as feminine as I would like and certainly not as feminine as I am, but pleasing to me nonetheless. But I'll get to that part of my story eventually.

My early life is a closed book to me. My mother died when I was still wearing diapers, and I was left to the tender care of a young married lady next door.

Finally my father must have observed that I was getting a dirty deal, because he married again. As far as I personally was concerned, it made little difference. My stepmother did take good care of me for a while.

As I grew in wisdom and stature, I formed many dear attachments with schoolmates, one especially close one with a certain girl who was about my own age, named Mary Ryan. We were almost inseparable, and would play by the hour and, even as we matured, indulge in all the childish games of youth.

In the early, playing-with-dolls days of my friendship with Mary, I noted that her girl dollies were different under their little outfits than I was under my garments. Mary concurred; she had noted the same thing. Their fronts were all monocolored, smooth and flat, while my top was curved and above my belly button (also missing from the dollies), where my waist tapered out, there was the outline of ribs and an intimation in the soft flesh of growing womanliness. Rising on my young upper torso were two hillocks of softness, crowned at the peaks with darker flesh that responded curiously to the touch of my fingers and sending waves of sensation coursing through my body.

Below the elastic waist of my generous bloomers, my dolly's body and mine differed radically, too. My body had hips while the doll's had none. My little hip bones showed themselves more with each maturing day. My legs became more shapely and, as I grew taller in spurts and flashes, long and lean thighs tapered to knees that turned out again in strong, lithe calves. These curved down to shapely ankles and perfectly proportioned feet and toes.

And between my legs! Where my doll was stitched together, I was split apart. I felt a smooth dome of supple young skin taut beneath my exploring hands, curving down to crevices I could not easily see but could readily touch. I could feel an opening that for months, probably years, I dared not penetrate deeper in my process of self-discovery. Yet as I matured, the structure there seemed to become more complex, a bud unfolding its petals in its metamorphosis to the full blossoming flower of womanhood. It invited exploration and enjoyment. It was only natural to appreciate the unfolding wonders of nature. So I did.

These things Mary and I discussed over the years in our childish innocence. We did not think them lewd or unspeakable as so many did—and still do. We shared the information and wonderment of our individual discoveries with one another in straightforward discussion, and grew both in wisdom and stature in the process.

About this time my stepmother had grown tired of my father, and it was common community gossip that she was "stepping out." At any rate, I was being left alone a great deal, and there were times that I would not have sight of my parents for several days at a time. We had a cook who prepared all of my meals, and, so long as I never went hungry, I did not waste much time in worrying about the antics of my parents.

This leeway gave me the chance to be alone with Mary. I am not at all sure just how we ever got started talking about ourselves, but in some way we started. Day after day our heads would come close together and we would talk over such things that many women never dreamed of.

Mary lived several blocks from our house. Her parents had never met my parents and did not know any of the gossip that was being circulated about my stepmother.

In fact, they seemed to feel that when Mary was with me, she was in the best of company. They would even give their permission for her to stay overnight at our house, little dreaming that their darling daughter and her friend were practically alone and free to do anything that their hearts might desire.

Of course, that in itself was not out of the ordinary. But Mary and I had fallen into habits that we needed to be alone to practice. It's clear to me now that those nights when we were left to ourselves—and the afternoons we spent in my room alone—went a long way toward molding my later sexual life. I will try and relate, as well as I can remember, the events leading up to this relationship.

It seems as if it was a very long time after we had become childhood friends that we started these things.

It was a rainy afternoon. Our outdoor study class had been cancelled and we had returned home. Thinking ourselves quite mature—we were in our late teens—we lounged in the storm-darkened room and chatted about our "childhood" days. As we were both still extremely innocent, we spoke of our dolls and their differences with our own anatomy. We reminisced about how we would pretend our dollies were ill and we doctored them to make them well again. Soon we tired of this foolish prattle, and I said to Mary, "You know, we've often talked about how our parts are different from our dolls, but not about how they are different one from the other."

To this not-very-veiled invitation, Mary responded, "Let's return to the old days of our tender youth and play sick as we did with our dollies. You be sick and I will be the doctor and make you well."

I acceded to this request at once, since it was a desirable change from the lifeless dolls, and said, "Oh yes, that will be fine. Doctor, I have a pain in my tummy and I wish that you would take care of me."

Mary took to her part at once. She had me lie back on the bed. Then she pulled up my dress and, unbuttoning my bloomers, she pulled them down, exposing my bare tummy. Placing a hand on my belly she rubbed it sturdily, kneading and tickling my flesh. I naturally squirmed under her hand. She bent down and, looking between my legs, observed my slit. Placing her hand now on this, she gave it a few rubs and pets.

I squirmed some more at this contact of her hand upon my most intimate part but, liking the feelings that she inspired within me, did not make any move at all to remove her roving hand.

"You have a nice little cranny," she said, still caressing it, "and if you like I will let you look at mine."

I thought that this was a good idea and told her so. We took off our drawers and examined each other in all sorts of postures and positions.

Because she had first taken the doctor role, Mary continued to dominate the exploration. Gently pushing me on my back again, she positioned herself kneeling at my feet, her hands on my ankles. My legs were stretched out straight, knees together and my passage tightly closed to touch and view. She grasped my ankles and pushed forward, causing me to raise my knees, still pressed together. This action had the effect of lifting my thighs and calves off the bed, and this inverted V exposed my moistening slit to the cool air, although not to Mary's view.

Mary inched forward on the bed and raised herself up off her haunches, each of her knees now outside each of my ankles. Her thighs were now apart so I could see her secret parts. I had barely glimpsed my own in all my years of awareness. She was lovely, the mound above her slit pulsing as she raised her hands to my knees. She held my feet held loosely between her knees and forced my knees apart and to the bed.

This caused me to shift my hips and opened me wide to Mary's view. I felt my netherlips part slightly and they flushed with warmth as the cool air touched them. I realized I would never really experience directly the wondrous view of myself that Mary now had of me. Then she ran her dainty young-woman's hand down the inside of my spread-eagled thighs and, with the ball of her hand, caressed my throbbing mound and cupped my gaping passageway.

Nearly driven to ecstatic distraction by this new sensation, I opened my eyes just a bit and saw Mary above me in an ecstasy all her own. Her head was thrown back, neck taut, her exquisite bud of a mouth parted ever so slightly and her eyes closed, eyelids exposed and dark beneath arched brows. Her hair brushed her shoulders as she rocked in a slow, gentle rhythm.

I became aware that, at the whole other end of my body, her slick and hot crotch was rubbing, lifting, sliding and rubbing against my still-pinned feet. This motion was transferred through her body and down her arm to the open palm pressing with increasing vigor against my spreading, slickening slit. As her body rose, heaved forward, and slid back, I saw more of the parts I had barely had the nerve to touch on my own person.

I had noticed that there was essentially no difference between us. The touch of Mary's hand upon me, seemed to thrill me and she told me that she also liked to have me feel her.

After playing so for a while, we became cautious, but decided that the next time we would explore still more. We put on our clothes again and called it a day.

The chance that we were awaiting came soon. Mary was given permission to stay overnight in my company. We lost no time, after my parents had retired, in getting to my room and throwing off all of our clothing. Mary was a beautifully formed creature in all of her innocent nudity. I don't recall how old we were then, but her body was developed far more than most girls of our acquaintance. Her hips were well rounded and plump, and her breasts had filled out so that you could see they would soon be the perfect globes of maidenhood.

Her cranny was smooth and soft, a cushion of mossy growth having formed above its lips, and these tender folds looked like a pink blush rose nestling between her silken thighs.

You may be sure that I was curious to examine her in full and to compare her charms with my own. We stood before a long mirror that was in my room and moved about to notice the play of the muscles in our legs, thighs and bellies. Then, as if acting upon common impulse, we ran to the bed. Leaping in, we grasped one another in our arms and lay quite still, content to feel the cool fleshiness of each other.

Mary was first to take the initiative. Taking my hand in her own, she placed it upon her cranny and at the same time began to pat me gently on my badge of sex.

I needed no urging to do to her as she was doing to me. We lay close together and a pleasant feeling came over me as I felt her naked body near to mine.

By this time Mary had located the opening of my slit and easily let her finger slip within me. For a moment I was unable to move, this violation coming so suddenly upon me. Cold—and then warm—shivers ran up and down my spine. I felt funny all over and my head seemed to grow hot. Without any intent on my part, I found my finger inside her. I was surprised with what ease I penetrated her.

While I was doing this, Mary was running her finger in and out of me and I seemed unable to control myself, feeling the most pleasant sensations coming over me. I wriggled and writhed in pleasure. Knowing that if she brought to life these feelings in me my finger would do the same for her, I shot my finger in and out of her and was delighted to see her move about as if in imitation of my actions.

I do not recall when we ceased this delicious mutual fingering, but eventually sleep overcame us. We slept like this, a finger deep in each other's slit, until awakening the next morning. We were grasped tightly in each other's arms, our lips trembling and trading sweet, avid kisses.

At every chance thereafter, we managed to carry out our little act of love. I do not believe that either of us knew just what we were about in this, but we seemed to act from some instinctive urge.

Mary told me that Edna, one of our classmates had run her hand up under Mary's dress one afternoon while they were in the toilet together. After patting her between the legs for a second, she had stuck her finger into Mary's slit and tickled her.

The girl had told Mary that the little hole she had at the bottom of her mount was her cranny. That was all Mary knew about it, and I, of course, only knew what I learned from her. (It must be obvious by now that we had been terribly sheltered.)

As time went on, we desired to add to our knowledge. Naturally, as we fully realized that what we were doing was something that was not to be told to our parents for any reason, the first person we thought of was the girl who had first fingered Mary.

I did not know Edna personally, so I had Mary introduce us. Then I invited her to come over to my house, preferably during some afternoon, as that was the best time.

Only a few days later, she told Mary that she could come visit. Both Mary and I, terribly excited, waited impatiently until school was dismissed.

We met our new partner and hurried toward my house. On the way, Mary blurted out that what she wanted to know was more about our crannies. Our would-be teacher burst out laughing and told us to keep quiet or someone might overhear. However, when we arrived at my house and she found out that there was no one at home and that we could go to my room and we would be alone with the door locked, she quickly agreed to tell us all that she knew about this interesting subject.

Seating herself on the bed, she told us that all ladies were built just like we were, possessing just such a cranny, which was called a cunt. Men had a thing like a sausage called a prick with a funny sac below it which contained the balls. She told us that when a man's prick was in a lady's cunt, it felt a whole lot better than our fingers.

Mary suggested that we all take our clothes off and play about a while. Edna, laughing, said that she was afraid that someone might come in and catch us. I proudly locked the door and told her that she need not fear. She looked at Mary, who by now had nearly all of her clothes off, then at me. I was undressing as quickly as I could. She hesitated a minute, but then unbuttoned her dress and joined us.

You may be sure that Mary and I watched her with wide eyes as she stripped. She was much bigger than we were, and although I was prepared for something different, I was astonished to find that Edna had a growth of dark hair on her cunt, quite unlike the golden fleece that patched both Mary and me. Examining it, I found it as soft as our womanly fur.

Her breasts, which she told me to call tits, were significantly larger than our own and had cute little red nipples. They were sticking out, hard as rocks, and I could hardly resist the impulse to bite each of them, then and there.

Edna seemed rather nervous when she had all of her clothes off before us. Mary and I ran around her and felt her backside and breasts and fingered her cranny. Laughing, she pushed us away, and said, "Why, you are worse than two boys, I believe. Here, I will fix you." She had both Mary and me lie on our backs on the bed and got on it between us, running a finger into each of us at the same time. She told Mary to do the same to her, and in that way the three of us worked at each other until we could stand it no longer and we had to rest. Of course, we didn't progress to orgasm because none of us quite knew that it was there awaiting us at the culmination of our youthful explorations.

Then, because she had broached the subject, we inquired of Edna what experience she'd had with boys and their stiff pricks. She admitted that she had very little firsthand knowledge of the mighty male weapon itself. She had, however, met a boy just two days ago whom she was sure would teach her, if she gave him a chance. He had grabbed her hand and had put it on something hard between his legs. When she did not get at all mad at this, he had pulled her to him and kissed her and told her that he would fuck her soon. She wasn't entirely certain what that meant, but she was sure that a prick had something to do with it.

The three of us spent the rest of the afternoon exploring each other. Finally, we got tired and dressed. Edna kissed us both and promised to tell us if anything happened that might be of interest.

It was several weeks, however, before she told Mary that if we wanted, she would come over to my house again. My father was out of town, and my step-mother was going away the next day. I told Mary to invite her for the following afternoon, and, if Edna made excuses at home, it would be possible for her to stay with us all night. She said that she would.

You may imagine that both Mary and I were crazy for the next day to come. We knew that we would learn more about the question of sex. Time never seemed to pass so slowly.

But finally the afternoon arrived, and with it our Edna, all smiles and laughter. "Well, Michelle," she said, addressing me as she kissed me, "at last I have got it. I got well fucked last night and am eager to tell you both all about it. Believe me, it is keen to have a boy's big prick stuck way into your cunt."

I was thrilled through and through at her smutty words, and once in the house I threw my arms around this pretty girl and my hand ran up to her cranny. My other hand went under my own dress as my own cunt was itching and twitching. I longed to have it cooled by one of my companions.

Edna took mercy on me and, raising my dress, she rubbed me on my spot. I was soon a little better. Without further loss of time we hurried to my room, and soon the three of us had all our clothes off. We hopped in the bed and, as we lay there fondling each other, Edna told us her story. As near as I can remember now, after all this time, it was as follows:

"I will tell it all to you from the beginning so that you will both understand just how it all came about. The other day, after I had left school, I met the boy who had made advances to me. He asked me if I wanted to take a walk down through the riverbed in back of his house.

"Of course I felt sure that I knew what he was after, and I was perfectly willing to go with him. After putting on a little bashful act about going alone down there with him, I consented.

"Sure enough, as soon as we got down in the riverbed and under the trees where we were out of the sight of any spectators, he began to get familiar with me. He stopped and said, 'Let's stay here a while.' I stopped. I looked at him and he came right up close to me and put his arms around me. He pressed his lips to mine in a clinging kiss.

"Oh, girls, if you only knew how I felt when he kissed me. It sent such thrills of bliss running up and down my spine and seemed to set me on fire. I just closed my eyes and let him kiss away. I leaned a little against him and he squeezed me and put one of his hands on the front of my waist. He squeezed and pressed my breasts and tickled the little tips till I thought that I would go mad.

"Then he dropped his hand. I felt it on my leg, squeezing and rubbing higher up my thigh till he found that I had on a pair of tight bloomers. He made a vile remark and withdrew his hand, pushing me away.

"I was very sorry that he took away his hand as I was feeling very good. You may be sure that is the last time I will ever wear bloomers, for I know that had he touched my cunt I would have felt even better. From now on I am going to be open and ready for the boys.

"Anyway, we were standing right in front of a clump of trees with a nice secluded spot under them. Giving me another chance, he grasped me by the hand and drew me under the trees. I said nothing, as I was perfectly willing to let him do as he liked. I noticed that there must have been others there before us, as the ground was covered with newspapers.

"He pulled me down on the ground in a sitting posture and sat down beside me, gathering me into his arms. He kissed me and squeezed my breasts. I put my arms around his neck and kissed him back. Then he put his hand up under my dress, which was easy as I had my legs wide open. He tried to force it under the elastic bands of my bloomers, but gave up in disgust when he saw it was impossible.

"I smiled at him and asked him if he wanted me to take them off. He quickly answered, 'Yes!'

"I rose to my feet and, lifting my dress, pushed my underthings down and stepped out of them. I was a little awkward in doing this in front of him. I then laid them beside me and sat down again. He put his arms around me again and kissed me.

"I kissed him back and felt his hand again on my thighs. It moved at once to my cunt and he pushed one of his fingers into me. For a few minutes we lay there, while he rubbed my cunt and I kissed him madly. I laid back a little, and he took one of my hands in his and placed it on the front of his pants and I felt that hard dagger leaping inside.

"It seemed much bigger than I had expected it to be, and I began to be a little afraid of what I had started. But he opened his pants with his free hand and let it jump out before I had time for a second thought.

"It was really nice looking, about four inches long, possibly an inch wide—that is two or three inches around. At first there was some skin that covered it all, hanging over the head, but when he saw that I was so interested in this strange thing, he proudly drew back this covering skin and exposed to my gaze a red, swollen head.

"'Is this the first prick that you have ever seen?' he asked, shaking it at me.

"I assured him that it was, and he twined my hand around it. I squeezed it and it seemed to get harder while I held it in my hand and examined it.

"'Do you know why I brought you here, Edna?' he asked, running his finger in and out of me until I thought I would die from pleasure. We could both feel the juices stirring in me, for his finger made a wet, squishy sound as it passed in and out of my cunt.

"I told him that I supposed that he wanted to fuck me, and if he would promise me that he would not hurt me, it was all right for him to go ahead.

"'It's a go, then,' he said, and he kissed me again. Holding me around the waist, he raised my dress up high. I did not want him to see me naked like that; it seemed different from letting him feel me with his hand under my clothes. But I didn't want him to stop again, so I said nothing. I know my face must have been fiery red from shame.

"Then his finger again ran into me, and he moved it about rapidly until a terrible shudder ran over me, and I thought I was dying.

"'Now, just a few minutes,' he said, 'and it will all be over. Let me lie between your thighs so that I can get at you, Edna,' he instructed, and at the same time he spread my legs wide apart. I did not say a single word.

"Then he grasped his hard shaft, and drawing the skin well back from the head, placed the bare tip of it at the entrance of my cunt.

"'Take it in your hand,' he said, 'and guide it to just where my finger has been. Make yourself as limp as possible as it will hurt you a bit at first. After that it will feel simply grand.'

"When he said that it was going to hurt me, I tried to get up. But he was right on top of me and it did me no good. At the same time he pressed his legs on my thighs and pushed with his prick. It banged against my belly and, being afraid that it might hurt me, I took hold of it in my hand and steered it straight at my hole as he had told me to do.

"I tried not to be afraid, but I was lying stiff, waiting to be hurt, instead of lying limp as he had told me. He gave a terrible push with his hips and a sharp pain shot through me as the rod was jammed into my cunt. I let out a yell and struggled with all of my might to get up again. He was strong and held me tight, and soon the terrible pain stopped and a wonderful feeling came over me. He wriggled a bit and jiggled his prick back and forth inside me.

"I cannot fully describe it, only that it felt like fainting with wonderful music playing and everything. Just as I was beginning to enjoy it the most, the sensations really starting to build, he pulled out of me and rolled over. White stuff squirted out of the head of his prick in a shower onto the grass.

"I was almost in tears with disappointment and asked him why he had stopped. He told me that if he had let that load shoot off inside of me it might make me pregnant. I told him that it was just beginning to feel good when he jerked it out, and he laughed, saying, 'I suppose you would like to have me put it back into your cunt.' 'Yes, yes,' I said, opening my thighs wide, not caring now if he saw me or not, 'do that please.'

"'Look,' he said, and I looked at his prick and it had shriveled away so that it was almost hidden in the hair of his belly. 'The next time,' he said, 'I will have a rubber, and then I can leave it inside of you. The rubber will keep the stuff from harming you. When we come down here again I will continue to pump in you. It was only for your own good and protection that I pulled out.'

"He made me promise not to tell anyone what we had done and seemed scared that I would. Then he kissed me and gave me a few hugs. Seeing that he was not going to do it again, I put on my bloomers and we started back home.

"Then, the day before yesterday, he told me that if I wanted it again, that he had a rubber with him. He promised that he would leave his prick in me. Of course I was perfectly willing, and we went to the same place. After we sat down and he put his hand under my clothes, he was surprised to find that I did not have on any bloomers.

"I told him that I would never wear bloomers again as I liked to be open and ready for petting. He said that was wonderful. He soon had his prick out and I grabbed it, as I was not afraid of it anymore. I pushed back the skin and rubbed it up and down as he seemed to like it. He stuck his finger in my cunt and as soon as I was hot, he pushed me on my back. With my hand guiding it, he soon had his prick stuck in me.

"This time it felt perfectly wonderful from the start, and I moved about under him as he pushed it in and out. I tell you, girls, there is nothing like a boy's prick to send thrills of delight through your soul.

"For a while he kissed me and pushed in and out of me while I lay there and enjoyed it. Then he pulled it out, put the rubber over it, and then put it back in.

"I was surprised to find how easily it went in me, but as I knew that I was all wet inside, that may have helped it. With the rubber on it, it didn't feel so warm and nice. He was soon wiggling back and forth so fast that I couldn't do anything but hold onto him with my legs and arms. Then, all of a sudden, he went limp and lay on me.

"'There, Edna, you got all of it that time. How did you like it?' he panted.

"'Oh,' I told him, 'please do it again. Do it all over again.' But all my begging and praying couldn't get him to get it hard again.That was all that I got."

While Edna had been telling her story, we had been fingering each other as fast as we could and were all burning with lust. Mary jumped up and said,

"I have an idea, girls. Why not get something shaped just like a boy's prick and use that on ourselves in place of our fingers?"

For a while we could not think of anything, but finally Edna suggested that bananas would be just the thing. We all ran downstairs naked as we were, and as luck would have it, we found a bunch. We brought them back to the bedroom.

After some talking, we decided that it would be best to leave the skins on as we were not sure if they were hard enough to stand up to what we planned if we peeled them.

We took a knife and trimmed the end where the stalk was, and then each of us put one in our cunts as far as we could. It felt funny at first, and then rather good, but got rather tiresome holding them there and working them in and out.

Then Edna suggested that Mary lie back on the bed so that she could get on top of her. Holding the banana tightly between her thighs, Edna proposed to take the part of a man and thus give Mary the pleasure of a masculine fuck. Anxious for the experience, Mary quickly complied, throwing her legs open and thrusting herself up to the awkwardly balanced Edna who was having difficulty holding the banana in place to service Mary. She also kept trying to insert the other end of the yellow fruit into her own cranny and was not having much success at either end.

Since the process was not going smoothly, I decided to help, knowing they would do the same for me. With Edna nestled in the valley between Mary's legs, I reached in from behind to take charge of the banana, allowing Edna to take her hand away and thus bringing the beautiful cunts of the two women closer together. They were soon pressed chest to chest on each other, four lovely, soft titties spread flat against one another, four arms outstretched above their heads, and their four hands clasped desperately together.

I reversed my direction and straddled above them, sandwiching Edna and pressing Mary deep into the mattress, though she did not object. My own steamy slit was slipping and sliding on Edna's arched spine as I worked the banana with both my hands and all the skill I could muster, up and down, in and out of their throbbing cunnies. As I inserted and extracted the phallic fruit, each girl heaved and moaned with pleasure. Their bucking and writhing stimulated the seat of my desires to white-hot passion.

I had a full view of Edna's humping rump and glistening slit. The dark rosebud of her anal opening was pulled into unencumbered view as my forearms spread her cheeks apart while I worked. As I heaved forward to do my duty with all diligence, my aching breasts pressed into the small of her back and that other opening fell to my lips. Puckering them as it was puckered, I kissed it warmly. Edna squealed and writhed with greater delight, and I plunged ahead with furious purpose to let my tongue taste, tease, and probe the taut bumhole.

When my turn came to be fucked in a manly way by Edna, she suggested I have mine doggy style, as she called it. I protested that I wished to be accorded all the honors Mary, had received, but Edna persisted in directing the effort in her own way. I assumed her position over the recumbent Mary who had drifted far away in her reverie following the flurry of her first almost-proper fuck. She lay completely relaxed beneath me, kissing me tenderly while our breasts brushed softly against each other. Edna shifted us down to the end of the bed but insisted I remain on my knees with my rump in the air while she stood behind with the banana held at crotch level just like a man's stiff tool.

Wanting to get fucked with this approximation of a prick, I did as I was told and was not disappointed by the experience. At first Edna gave up the manly pose and, dropping to her knees, ran her hands up and down my back, thighs, and buttocks from the nape of my back to the back of my knees. As she rose and fell, her breasts brushed against me; I could feel their weight as they stroked downward, and their size and length as they pulled up against my skin. Mary had recovered some and her hands soon found my tits swaying above her. They cupped and molded about my dangling pendants, and I returned the touch to Mary, turning my head to kiss her softly on the mouth, our darting tongues meeting.

As we tongued each other hotly, Mary's hands moved to pinch my rubbed-red nipples between her thumb and index finger. A flurry of mixed sensations rushed through me: curious and briefly distracting pain at the momentary pinch, then the rising heat of passion as the pinch subsided into numbness and my areola contracted and hardened. The very tips of my tits, held firmly in Mary's loving grasp, got as hard as little pebbles.

This passion played out in its own way for Edna at my exposed bottom. Sensing the animal emotions being released, and equally caught up in the sexual tumult, she pressed hot, flickering tongue-kisses into my jumping slit. She nestled her nose against my distended rump opening. Then she moved her tongue to the anal hot spot, returning the favor I had given to her, running it around the sensitive rim, pressing it gently just a tiny way into the never-before-violated opening.

Then something different caressed my upraised parts. Not the banana certainly—the fleshy coverage was too great and the penetration barely at all. I disengaged from my kissing of Mary long enough to turn my head and look. Edna held her breasts in her hands and was rubbing them, pressing them, massaging them against my passion-slacked, saliva-drenched lovelips. After pleasuring me and herself thusly, she cupped and lifted her glistening orbs to her lips. To my surprise, she was able to kiss and suck them fully to near where they darkened. I was amazed that she could reach out her pointy tongue, the tongue that had so recently been in my cunny and rumphole, to taste the mixture of bodily delights dripping at the tips of her nipples.

"Oh, Edna, Edna," I cried out at the sight of her lost in her own delight, "fuck me now, fuck me like you said you would. Fuck me like you fucked Mary. Fuck me like a man fucks a woman."

Brought back to the here and now, Edna smiled, took a step back, and picked up the long-abandoned banana. Taking it in her right hand, she placed her left palm on the tip of my spine. Letting her thumb slip down to press against the button of my asshole, she drew up my flesh and pulled my slit tight by the action. The curved banana held like a pistol, she inserted just the tip into my lust-crazed opening. Working it about high in the hole, she let it go a bit deeper and deeper with each thrust, pressing it upward toward my spine.

I nearly wept with pleasure and desire. In her motions she unleashed all manner of sensation. But she neglected the engorged button at the front of my womanly gateway.

How foolish of me to think that Edna would have abandoned me so. After several longer and deeper strokes toward my rump, Edna rolled the fruit forward, sliding its length along the length of my slit. She touched my clit with the tip of the banana, then inserted the pricklike tool nearly fully into my hot box. She rubbed and twisted the deep-sunk phallus against my joy button while her thumb teased the front of my opening and her other hand worked my bumhole and the back end of my slit. All the while Mary was clamped onto my tits with grasping hands like lobster claws. Finally I exploded in a rush of passion, knowing the full extent of pleasure.

With all the wiggling and contorting and contracting, the noble banana finally split its skin, turning to mush inside me. The major outburst having exhausted us, Mary and Edna took turns licking and sucking the fruit's sediments from my passage, and I got a taste from their lips.

That was my first experience in being fucked. That, of course, was by a girl. However, I made up my mind that I was going to have the real thing the first chance I had.

CHAPTER TWO

II

Time went on, and Mary and I were still permitted to spend our time together as much as we wished. We had tried every way possible to get hold of a boy to fuck us, but so far had met with nothing but dismal failure. We had tried also all sorts of objects to fuck each other with, but we finally decided that bananas were of the best shape.

One day we had a wonderful idea. We went down to one of the department stores and bought some of the artificial fruit that they have on sale there, making sure that there were two bananas among the assortment. This artificial fruit, that is sometimes left on a table as a decoration, was made out of some kind of wax and worked fine, so we worried no more over disposing of the mashed fruit that used to result after a hard frigging on our part.

Mary and I both finished our year's study at the same time, and I hoped that we would continue our experiences together but I was disappointed. It was decided to send me to Los Angeles where I was to stay and study all of the time.

The day finally arrived when I was to depart. With a good many heartaches, I bade my friend Mary a tearful goodbye and Father took me away.

In Los Angeles I was assigned to a room with a very pretty girl who seemed younger than myself in years and experience. For several weeks I was pretty busy, getting started on my lessons.

However, it was not long before I began wishing to feel the touch of something, anything between my thighs. After going to bed I would try to satisfy myself with my finger, and took great care that my roommate would not discover me in the throes of pleasure.

One night when I had been lusting all day, I went to bed early, as I had obtained a banana and hoped to use it before Betty, my roommate, came in. Just about the time that I had reached the hottest point in my pokings, the door opened and in she walked.

I do not know if she had suspected my activities before this but, to my surprise, she came over to the bed where I was lying and kissed me with her lips. Well, as you may imagine, that almost set me off. Then, drawing away, she commenced to undress.

In a moment she was standing before the mirror looking at herself, admiring her beautiful form. I did not blame her for this at all because she truly had something to admire.

As I had observed her in her clothing, Betty had

appeared to me immature and naive. But as she slowly undressed before me, I realized I had either been blinded by my own self-absorption or had been fooled by her modest clothing.

Betty was a beautiful girl, ripe with the promise of full womanhood, seething with latent sexuality and pent-up passion. As she slipped out of her prudish cardigan and tightly buttoned, stiffly pressed blouse, her breasts fairly burst out above the encumbrance of her brassiere. As she unbuttoned the back of her calf-covering plaid skirt and stepped out of it and her slip in one move, she revealed a finely toned and sculpted body. She was statuesque—that was the word that came immediately to my mind, although until that moment I don't think I knew what the term meant to me.

Standing there in her bobby sox, saddle shoes, generous bloomers, and protective bra, she was beautiful. How had I missed it all the time we had been roommates? Clearly she was aware of her beauty. And she was aware of me. How could I have been so unaware?

I could see both her back and her front now reflected in the mirror, and I could also see her steal a glance at me. I looked at my own reflection and saw that I was staring in awe and appreciation. Betty's response was cool. Reaching around behind her back, she unhooked the monstrous bra that held her enormous breasts in check. But she did not remove it right away, the little tease. Instead, her back still to me but her frontal reflection fully available in the mirror, she let it hang over those liberated globes while she played about under its cover.

Running her hands down and then up her sides, she gently brushed the sides of her fine tits as if to restore the circulation. She cupped them in her palms, thumbs teasing the nipples, all beneath the cover of that undergarment-armor which blocked my view. She rotated each breast in a different direction and I saw them, in reflection, peek from the top, then the side, then the bottom of the barbarous brassiere. Finally extending her arms straight out in front of her, she shrugged her shoulders forward and the unhooked chastity shield fell away from her breasts to reveal two lovely volcanoes peaked by a lava flow of dark crimson flesh. Her nipples were broad and smooth, and her caresses had brought them to large peaks clearly discernible in the reflection. She brought her outstretched arms above her head and the orbs reshaped into magnificent pears. Between her upraised arms, Betty tilted her head to admire her reflection and smiled softly to herself. And to me, I hoped.

Still in her bobby sox and brown and white saddle shoes, she grasped the waist of her oversized bloomers. Finally, I thought, she would pull them down and I'd be afforded the sight to which I felt I was now entitled. But I was wrong.

Betty did the complete opposite of what I expected. Thumbs hooked at the elastic waist of her garment, she gathered the material at each leg in her hand and pulled it in and up toward her slit. I was dumbfounded. All the pure white cloth she gathered and pulled together until a taut, narrow band of material sheathed her most intimate slit. I, and she, could both see the full length of her legs to her hips and the easy undulations of her hipbones and belly, her womanly mound, and curving thighs. Holding the gathered garment in one hand now, she slowly moved it left and right, clearly manipulating and pleasuring the unseen treasures beneath the cloth.

Her free hand wandered about her breasts and belly, then back again to her crotch. In the shadow where I could not clearly see, she reached beneath the sheltering cloth and spread her slit open to take the dry white material between her cunt lips. A thin band of white, accentuated by the dark bush that glorified her mound and labia, was drawn tight into her. Glowing, curving flesh spilled around that pristine strip.

The free hand wandered again to her belly, her breasts, then down her side to her waist. Reaching around her back, she gathered the material of her pant legs and pulled it taut up her crack, exposing her firm and lovely buttocks to my view. I didn't know where to look first—at the reflected glory in front, or the living, glowing, rosy flesh behind, burning for a touch, a kiss, a caress. Pulling up with both hands, then gently pushing, then pulling the material—could it be?—tighter still into her, I thought Betty would fairly split herself in two before I had a chance at her. Her eyes closed in ecstasy and she moaned softly to herself. She raised up on her toes—still in her ankle socks and brown and white shoes—and all the muscles in her legs and buttocks, back, breasts, and belly took on new and glorious shape.

It made me hot to look at her. As though she was aware of my thoughts, she turned to me, and in doing so exposed to me her lovely front. She was trying to entice me through sheer passion to grab her and pull her to me.

Then she again came close to the bed and, bending over me, kissed me in an electric manner. Well, to make a long story short, when she did that I could not help myself, even if I were to die for it on the spot. I placed my hand on her soft fur and twined my fingers in it.

Like a shot, she sprang into the bed beside me and, as quick as lightning, her hand slipped down to my grotto. Finding the spot she desired, her hand came in sudden contact with the banana that was still buried within me, and she almost screamed in amazement and fear.

"Michelle, what is it, are you a man? Tell me quickly if you are a man, or are gifted with a prick like one. If you can fuck like one, fuck me and fuck me quick, as I have been dying for it and have been afraid to say anything."

Throwing off the covers, I let her see that I was just a girl like her own sweet self, but that the object that she had taken for a prick was capable of satisfying her after a fashion.

"Well," Betty said, "you're not a man, I am sorry to see. But with that tool you use I think from now on I'll address you like a man. Michelle…M…Mi… Michael. No, Mike. I like that much better. Mike it is.

"Well, Mike," she said, evidently disappointed that I didn't really have a prick for her, "I have something far better than that banana. Wait until I get it." Jumping out of bed, she unlocked her trunk and soon found a metal box which she brought back to the bed.

"Look, Mike," she said, "my father presented me

with this and told me that if I ever felt like I wanted a boy, I should resist the urge. But if the impulse got too strong, I was to take this and put it inside of me and work it in and out of me until I felt relieved.

"I used it several times before I left home but have been afraid to try it here as you were in the room. I did not know if you would approve. My parents are very open-minded and are not like other people."

As she was talking, she opened the box with a key and took out a hard rubber thing that looked a good bit like the banana I had, only larger and more round.

"This is a perfect rubber prick, just like a man's," Betty said. "I think that both of us, judging from your actions, dear, can make good use of it!"

With that said, she strapped the thing to her lithe and lovely loins as it also had a harness clearly made for the purpose. Thus equipped, Betty became a curious sight, for the moment more deserving than I to be called Mike. I was befuddled by the mix of emotions I felt—afire with desire for her feminine body so tantalizingly displayed for me, yet drawn by the sight of the stiff-standing tool now presented for my pleasure.

Betty approached, sinuous as a cat and oddly threatening with the rigid replica of manhood supported in her right hand. With one smooth motion, she extracted the banana from my already well-lubricated slit and tossed it aside. Holding me open with her free thumb and forefinger, she placed the smoothly capped head of the sturdy-veined pole between my cunt lips at the edge of the tight love channel.

"Now, Mike my laddie, or should I say lady," Betty growled, lowering her voice, "let's have at that pretty pussy you've been keeping all to yourself." And letting go with her hand, she arched her back and gave a joyous thrust to her hips. She impaled me in one swift motion on that blunt dagger lashed over her equivalent opening.

Fireworks exploded between my legs and in my head. The tool was honestly man sized I now know. Not as threatening as some, not as delicate an instrument as others it has been my pleasure to encounter, but more than adequate at that time to stretch the walls of my novice passage and reach parts as yet unfulfilled by the fingerings and fruit I had experienced to date.

Betty obviously sensed this and did her utmost to drive home her love-toy with vigor. She accompanied her pumping and grinding, thrusting and rotating, with deep guttural growls that at first frightened, then amused me, so bestial were they. She pumped me well, in much the same fashion as a man would, had one been in her place. She drove the dildo in to its full length, then withdrew it so that only the bulbous head remained within my nook. She alternated her strokes with slow rotations of her hips, so that the thick, blunt instrument stretched the sensitive membranes of my cunny and made the next probing plunge even more delightful and intense. I could feel the stirrings of passion deep within my belly and began to push back against her to speed the rising tide of pleasure that would soon engulf me. As she arched above me, her breasts dangling as she drove her hips in and out, I could see through the heat of my passion that she was coming as I was, although no tool was plunged in her wanton slit. Her pleasure fired mine, and I responded to her efforts with thrusts and dainty little moans of my own. We peaked simultaneously, and then Betty collapsed onto me and lay trembling with passion in my arms. We both panted wildly, scarcely able to catch our breath.

Of course I had to do for her what she had done for me, and you may believe me when I say we made good use of that wonderful imitation of the thing we dreamed of. To some people this may seem very crude, especially for two girls not yet experienced with the wider world. But you must consider that it was the only way that we knew of satisfying the desires that burned within us.

We both longed for boys and the feel of a real prick. But we had no way of getting any, so we had to do the best that we could with what we had at hand.

I was delighted to find that Betty was of the same disposition as myself, and more so to find an object that would not mush or melt in my cunt. Many a royal battle we had with her cunt-provoker, as she laughingly called it.

One night one of the girls in the school came into our room. She seemed older than us, and she was fine looking. Her name was Gladys. She had pictures of a man and a woman loving each other, and she showed them to us, asking if we didn't wish that we had a prick in us like that in the pictures.

We both agreed that we wished that we had, flashing knowing glances at each other. Then Betty goosed her, and I put my hand up under her dress and found that her cunt was moist.

"Uh oh," she said, pulling away from both of us and laughing. "I see that you girls are not at all backwards in receiving company. You certainly know how to use your hands. But understand we are talking about pricks, not jerking each other off."

"If you really want it, Gladys," said Betty, "we can give you a bigger prick than that one in the pictures, can't we Mike?"

"Oh, yes," I said. "It is only rubber, but I'll wager you, Gladys, that it will make you dance."

"Oh, let me see it, let me see it," she said. "I have never seen one. I have heard of them, but I have never seen one with my own eyes."

Betty got it out and Gladys examined it. She threw up her dress and showed us her pretty naked thighs, then pushed the tip of it into her cunt. "It feels like the real thing," she said. "Where on earth did you get it?"

Betty told her about her father giving it to her and, seeing how eager Gladys seemed to try the device, she began to undress.

Gladys and I had our own clothes off in a second, and the three of us leaped into bed. Betty had strapped the prick onto her loins, and we soon had Gladys's thighs spread wide apart. Betty climbed on top of her belly and stuck the prick into her cunt. Betty then worked her as she had me. She plunged the dildo in harshly and began thrusting with long, forceful strokes. She grasped Gladys's buttocks from underneath and pulled the girl to her each time she pressed forward, burying the rubber prick even more deeply. As she did this, she bent her head and ran her teeth over the rosy tip of one of the girl's tits, then tugged on the nipple until it stood up straight and wine dark. The other globe she left to me, and I fell to with gusto. I tweaked the nipple with my fingertips before lashing it with my tongue. I swirled around the tip and then used back and forth strokes to awaken the now-turgid flesh. Poor Gladys! Soon she was writhing with pleasure and in a few minutes lay back on the bed in a faint.

As soon as she came to, she cried "Oh, Betty, did you come too? Quick, let me have it," and while I watched, entranced, she turned herself around in the bed, crawled under Betty who was lying on her stomach, and put her face between Betty's thighs. I saw her tongue dart out of her mouth and into Betty's cunt, in and out like a stiff little poker, until Betty began to show signs of fainting herself.

Gladys jumped up and thrust the rubber prick in her own slit, working it violently back and forth until I thought she would push a hole in herself. Finally she stopped—I saw her tremble and I knew she was melting.

She then strapped it on and told me to open up, which I did. Guiding it straight as an arrow, she forced it up my cunt. Then, with increasing violence, she withdrew and pushed it in again and again until I was forced to surrender to my passion.

As she finished, and I lay on the bed panting with exquisite pleasure, she placed herself on the bed over me with her head by my mount and her crevice right over my panting lips. Again she attacked a cunt with her tongue—my own slit this time.

For a moment I wavered, and then my tongue darted out and into her trembling cunt. I tasted the sweet juice of womanhood for the first time in my life.

It gave me quite a thrill to think that I was sucking a girl's cunt, and I pressed my own slit down on Gladys's pistonlike tongue. She, as if in answer to my actions, put her own organ to my mouth, and I was nearly smothered by its wet embrace.

I determined to make her pay for that and dashed away with my tongue within her until I felt the hot wells open and close convulsively and a thin stream of her life shoot out and down my throat. I, in turn, besprayed her until, exhausted and panting, we lay side by side, head to tail on the bed.

I rather liked the feeling of her thighs about my head. Later on, as I shall tell, I often longed for the thrilling feel of a girl's nude legs around my neck.

"That is what we call milking," Gladys told me. "Most all of the girls love to do it and have it done to them. It's very nice to have it done to you, but I like your rubber prick much better. At any rate, it is nice to have both to amuse us. I think you are two lovely girls, and I know that we are going to have loads and loads of fun together."

With that observation, she warmly kissed both Betty and me, put on her pajamas and her coat, and left the room. After indulging in another bout with the prick, Betty and I fell sound asleep in each other's arms.

There is not much use in going over the doings of the next stretch of time. Suffice it to say that, although most of the girls tried at every chance to get boys, most of us were out of luck and had to be satisfied the best we could with our own means of obtaining pleasure.

One of the girls in our club went on a ride after, or

rather, during a dance one night, and the boy she was with gave her a rousing good fuck. However, it was noticed that she was gone from the dance and she was nearly expelled for it. After that, none of us dared try to go away during a dance and, unfortunately, that was the only time that we had a chance of meeting the boys.

Before leaving my memories of those days, I must tell you about our club. I think it was like most girls' clubs of the times. For the initiation, we made a girl strip naked and lie on a bed. Then we would fuck her good with the rubber prick or any other substitutes that we happened to have handy.

My father had become fairly well-to-do now, and I was given permission to move out of the school dorm to any housing I might select. So Betty and I made arrangements to rent a nice apartment just across from the campus. We quickly made some good friends. About three weeks after we had settled in, both Betty and I were invited to a party at Bob's apartment.

Bob was one of the most popular boys at school, and we felt that we were being honored by the invitation. Bob and his friend Jack called for us in Bob's car.

Bob seemed to have all kinds of money and he certainly knew how to spend it. We had a nice dinner at the party and plenty of liquor flowed. By the time we were through eating, most of the girls were quite lightheaded.

Then the boys turned on the radio and we danced for a while, but Bob quickly tired of this. He danced me into the next room and started necking with me. He didn't have any idea that he was the first man who had been this familiar with me. I did my best to make him think that I was wise and knew all about it.

His kisses burned me and I gave in to him passionately, running my hands through his hair and hugging him as hard as he hugged me. He put his hand on my tits and bounced them about. I did not attempt to stop him, and he soon had my dress unhooked and pulled down over one shoulder. Unfastening my brassiere, he bared my tits to his gaze. Then he grabbed them and squeezed them, petted, caressed, and kissed them. He raved over them, saying that they were the most perfect pair he had ever seen.

You can imagine the effect of all of this on me. I did not know if he was as passionate as I was, but I did know that if he wanted at that very moment to push me over and fuck me, he could have done it.

For that matter, he might as well have, for I saw a couple on the couch across the room from us kissing and hugging, and the boy had the girl's dress up so far that I could see her naked bottom, and he had his hand where I was wishing Bob would put his on my body.

Bob saw that I was watching the other couple and suggested that we have another drink. He took his straight, and I took a small one. Then I started to go back to the main party, but it seemed he had another idea. Opening a door in the hall, he pushed me into a bedroom.

There was someone in there, but we saw at once that it was Jack and Betty. Jack was working her up in good fashion. His hands were all over her tits, and her clothes were half pulled off her.

They both were well pickled. Seeing them, Bob started to back out, but I laughed and told him that we might as well stay as Betty and I had no secrets from each other.

Although I had never been through it before, I knew then that I was going to be fucked. Bob pulled me over to the bed and laid me down alongside the other couple. He threw himself down beside me, took me in his arms, and kissed and hugged me till I was burning with passion.

He soon had my dress unfastened. His hands were busy with my various charms, and I thrust them up to him to give him more play.

"If you want to save your dress so that it will look decent, you had better remove it, dear Michelle," said Bob, kissing me again.

"Right," I said merrily. Springing from the bed, I tore it off and then jumped back to be held fast in my lover's arms. I wanted to see his prick at once, but I was not sure whether I should reach out and take it out of his pants myself. But after he had put his finger far into my cunt and I wriggled on it, I lost all my sense of shame. I reached my hand over to the front of his pants, unbuttoned his fly, and let his prick jump out. It was almost like Betty's rubber one, only warm and pulsing with life. It was about six inches long and possibly a little thicker than the rubber imitation.

There was no skin over the head, which was quite red and larger than the body of it. His balls were nice and large as I juggled them around in his sac. Feeling them slipping through my fingers, warm feelings thrilled through my body. Bob continued to finger-fuck me, using all of the length of his finger in quick pushes. I pressed my cunt about his digit and almost swooned with the pleasure he gave me.

He pressed his lips to mine and his tongue went into my mouth. I did the same in a heaven of pleasure. This was nothing like the rubber prick, or even Betty or Gladys. I found that it was a lot different to be handled by a man, and I experienced feelings I had never thought possible.

From the hardness and the jumpiness of Bob's prick, I knew that he was ready and waiting to fuck me. And I, desiring it as much as he did, pressed my bare belly to his shaft.

Finally Bob gently eased me upon my back and placed himself over me, between my widely spread thighs. I had no fear at all of him hurting me. Taking his lovely prick in my hand and giving it a few squeezes, I steered it straight toward the mouth of my cunt.

As he slowly let his body drop onto mine and his prick slipped into me, I felt thrill after thrill spinning through my body. My brain reeled and I wrapped my arms around his neck and wiggled under him.

We lay still for a few moments, then Bob raised himself up and began to thrust with little movements of his hips. The sensations this caused were delightful and excruciating, like little ticklings that sent shivers through my entire body. My ecstasy became uncontrollable, however, when Bob became serious about his work. He started to use longer and deeper thrusts, penetrating to the core of my cavern with the entire length of his prick and leaving me breathless with each stroke. As he increased the length of his strokes, he increased the force as well, so that it wasn't long before his heavy balls were slapping my upturned buttocks as he buried himself inside me. And when he brought his hands up and supported himself by grasping my heaving tits, I thought I would very well die from the intensity of the emotion that swept over me!

Oh, it was certainly grand, that first fuck, and I really do believe that we kept it up for over half an hour before he began to increase his movements. I felt myself coming again and again. My cunt opened and closed like a hand squeezing his prick and then, at the apex of all my emotions, I felt a load of something hot pulsing and boiling into me, and I realized that he had come.

In all of my experience with the girls and their fingers and tongues, and the banana, and even with Betty's dildo, I had never been treated to this internal shower of masculine passion. It thrilled me to the core and my juices flowed with unrestrained delight as if to answer this outpouring of delicate cream.

My now extraordinarily lubricated channel wanted Bob harder and deeper still inside me. I wanted him to pound his spewing manhood up into me, up, up into my heaving chest. I wanted his hot, stiff prick inside me where I could clutch it forever—where I could endlessly hold it and pump it and milk it of its sticky essence.

I drove harder and harder in response to Bob's thrusting. The bone at the top of my passage ground hard against his pelvis. His tool was buried so deep inside of me it was as if we were one. The fleshy sac that hung beneath his erect manhood touched my raging rump, then left, then touched, then left again. How wonderfully equipped men were for giving pleasure. How willing I was to be pleasured by a stiff prick. With all these feelings overwhelming me, I slipped into a sublime darkness.

My next memory was that Bob's thrusting and driving had ceased, although his erect but waning tool was pleasantly resting in my passage. His face was closer to mine, his weight heavier on me than I remembered at the height of our passion, but it was not unpleasantly crushing.

"Hello," he breathed quietly at me. "Are you okay?"

"Okay?" I queried. "I'm better than okay. I'm excellent."

"That you are," Bob rejoined, and eased himself off and out of me. I groaned at the loss of that lovely rod of flesh between my legs. I closed my eyes again and drifted away on the memory for a moment, perhaps longer, I'm not sure. When I opened my eyes again I found Bob watching Betty and Jack. Jack was on top of Betty, her clothes all up in the air, naked to her waist. Jack was trying to get his prick into her but he was just drunk enough to miss the hole every time. She knew enough, however to grab hold of his prick and steer it into her slit.

I turned to Bob and told him to help Jack out instead of standing there laughing at them.

"Do it yourself," he laughed.

Not at all averse to feeling Jack's stalwart prick, and not without a few squeezes on my own part, I took firm hold of it; then I pulled open Betty's cunt and, placing the head within, allowed him to run it up into her.

Bob and I watched them. They bounced and danced on the bed; Jack gave my friend Betty a royal fuck. I thought that he was going to bore a hole in her the way he pushed and pounded. But Betty threw herself up to meet him and enjoyed every shove of his ramrod.

Finally I saw her eyelids flutter, and he gave one drive up in her and a terrible grunt. I knew by their actions that he was soaking her with his sperm the same as Bob had done to me. After a minute or two Jack rolled off of her, and she lay on the bed as though dead, her dress still up and her thighs spread wide so that you could see her cunt all red and open and wet.

Betty's dress was a sight, all rumpled, creased, and wrinkled, but I did the best that I could to make her look presentable. Then Bob and I went out to where the others were dancing. There was a couple almost fucking there on the davenport, and Bob made them go into the bedroom.

"Go ahead and fuck," he said, "but do it in there on the bed."

The couple laughed and arose, the girl's face flushed, her lips trembling, her eyes glistening with the feeling that she was experiencing. I stole a look at the front of the boy's pants and saw a big swollen lump. I knew that she had something coming to her.

They walked unsteadily to the room, and I, on pretense of shutting the door after them, left it open a crack. Peeking in, I saw him throw her on the bed and tear open his pants, throwing up her skirt and blouse.

He rolled her onto her stomach and pulled her to the end of the bed, onto her knees, much as Edna had done to me during my first experience with the banana. But what he proffered for the pleasure of this fortunate young lady with her legs spread, her rump high in the air at the end of the bed, was no ordinary golden fruit. It was a masculine weapon of considerable size.

I had misjudged the lump in his pants on the conservative side, that was for sure. Not that it had length—that it did not have in abundance. But its girth and veined surface! The cudgel he had in his hand now, which I could appreciate in all its glory but which was unseen by the about-to-be recipient, was breathtaking. It looked at a distance as if the lucky lad had a third, well-muscled arm growing between his legs—a third arm finished with a clenched and knuckled fist beyond its thick wrist.

With little ceremony the fellow took a step closer to his paramour and placed the head of his battering ram at her gates of pleasure. It nearly overwhelmed her outermost entryway. Clearly when he drove forward and introduced her to the fullness of this extra arm, it would test the walls of her queen's chamber. But apparently she was aware of his prowess and longed for it. I longed for it as well, from my secret vantage point.

He had barely laid his ramrod upon her when she gave her sweet ass a wiggle and backed down upon that thick, gnarled shaft with a vigor I would have thought impossible if I had not seen it with my own eyes. My own little tormented cunny twitched with delight at the sight of that stump enveloped by the tortuously stretched cunt. That she took charge in pleasing her man pleased me, too. It was a lesson for me, I concluded.

She backed down harder still and took him fully into her. I gasped and he heard me, looked over, smiled, then returned his attention to his sweetie. She writhed and twisted on that shaft as he bore harder into her. I heard her grunt with effort and then saw her loins flex once again as she took all of him as deeply as he could reach. He humped on, driving, extracting himself slightly, then driving again as she answered his every thrust. She was an inspiration. I shut the door softly and left them to their pleasures.

Finding Bob, I enjoyed a couple of dances with him, and after we had some more drinks, the boys drove Betty and me home. In the car we took advantage of the opportunities to feel each other and massage and tickle until we almost squirted. Bob wanted to give it to me again, but I told him no, and told Jack not to fuck Betty who was almost unconscious from the effects of liquor.

The next morning Betty had a wonderful hangover. I felt fine.

"You simply drank too much, my dear girl," I told her. "I wager that you do not even know who fucked you last night."

"Oh, Michelle," she said, "I would never have let anyone do it to me." She argued up and down that no one did. But when I showed her the stains on her underwear, she began to get frightened. Then I told her what Bob and I had done, and how I had watched her and Jack, and how she had been well fucked.

"Oh, Mike," she said, "to think that I had a prick within me and cannot even remember it."

"Well, you had it all right," I said, "and the way that you wiggled under it showed that you liked it well enough."

"Well," she said, "that should serve as a lesson to us both that we are never to get drunk. What if you had been drunk too? That would have been simply terrible. Both of us might have missed all the fun."

I agreed with her and we promised each other that from now on one of us must remain sober.

We saw Jack and Bob several times during the week but no mention was made on either side of what had taken place that night at their apartments. However, on Friday Bob phoned us and asked us if we wished to go to a wild party.

Of course it is unnecessary to say that we were perfectly willing and eager to go, and we agreed to meet them on the appointed night.

CHAPTER THREE

III

At nine o'clock Bob and Jack called for us. It took an hour to get to the house where the party was to be held, in a place near Balboa Beach.

It was a private home, and there were fifty or sixty people there before we arrived. There was plenty of booze, and I took care to give Betty a warning nudge and told her to slow down on that.

About midnight, everybody was feeling quite grand, and someone suggested that we all take a dip in the inviting surf.

Without further ado, everyone began to strip off their clothes, and soon we were completely naked and running up and down the sand on the edge of the water. At first I waited, but everybody seemed determined to go in. I quickly dropped my dress and other clothing.

Bob grabbed me by the arm and we ran after the rest of the bunch. We plunged into the water and had a great time playing about and splashing. Then I noticed that couple after couple began to slip slyly back to the house. I told Bob that I was getting cold, which was a fib. He took me by the arm and we started back.

I noticed that there were several couples who had stopped on the sandy beach to satisfy their passion—I could see male bottoms moving up and down over female bellies—but as far as I was concerned that was not for me. I had no intention of getting sand in my crack.

We ran to the house, and I noticed that the lights had been turned low. A number of the couples sat necking.

Bob and I quickly found a place on a soft rug behind a sofa, and we no sooner settled there than he took me in his arms and we kissed and hugged.

The booze that I had guzzled along with my own natural warm feelings and the contact of this agreeable nude hunk of manhood had the effect of heating me up so that I panted and longed to be impaled on his prick.

As for Bob, his cock had been as hard as a rock for the last hour. Taking it in my hand, I squeezed and pulled it while he rummaged about my cunt until we were both smoking with longing.

I allowed him to mount me. He placed the head of his prick at my cunt and drove it into me. I wiggled about beneath him and, as soon as he was fully within me, I poured a good load of my love juices down his plunger.

He pumped me for a good five minutes. After that he was not long in coming and, as he shot into me, I thought that I would swoon with pleasure. It seemed even nicer than when he had done it the Saturday before, and I began to feel very tender toward him.

We stayed at this place all night and Bob must have had me at least four times. I don't clearly remember where we stayed in the house. I know that I awoke in the morning in Bob's arms and, feeling his prick thumping against my bare belly, I immediately put it where it would do the most; we had another delicious bout of love.

After we finally arose we found Jack and Betty, who had been amusing themselves the same way we had. Then Bob, Betty, Jack, and I drove up to Long Beach and spent the day there playing about. We had lots of fun and late that evening we returned to our own apartments where the boys insisted that they were going to sleep all night with us.

After we had sat around a bit and we sang and danced to the radio, Bob took all of my clothes off and tumbled me into bed. He quickly stripped himself and was in beside me. He gave me a splendid poke and Jack and Betty came in naked and climbed into the bed with us. Jack gave Betty a fucking that shook the bed. Of course, Bob and I got all heated up over this and we kissed and embraced as Jack continued to poke Betty. Bob's prick was soon as hard as an iron rod.

I kissed and felt Betty while she was getting it and also put my hand between her and Jack so that I could feel him pounding it into her. After he had come, we dried ourselves. Bob took me in his arms and whispered: "I think, Michelle, that considering the way you felt Jack's tool when he was giving it to Betty, you would like to have him ram you for a change, while I give Betty a taste of mine."

"Oh, Bob," I pouted, "you are tired of me already. I thought that you would act that way. I knew that once you fucked me you would want another girl." With that said, I reached down and squeezed his prick.

He laughed and kissed me, and said, "I know, Mike, that you are just trying to be polite. But you know that you also are just like me and that a change of pricks would be in no way distasteful to you, am I not right?"

I hesitated to answer, as what Bob had said was perfectly true. My feel of Jack's wonderful cock had instilled within me a desire to experience that big prick banging my vaginal walls. But I wanted to be nice about it, just as Bob had said, and knew that Betty, on her part, felt the same as I did.

As I thought these things but said nothing, Bob touched Jack on the shoulder. Crawling away from me, Bob took Jack's place. He took Betty in his arms, began kissing and hugging her and feeling her tits. Jack was not at all bashful at this change. He kissed me and I immediately felt his rammer banging my belly. I was squeezing its head while he fingered my cunt, and I was soon hot as hell.

He climbed on top of me and stuck it in. When at the same time Bob mounted Betty, I felt a little twinge of jealousy. But prick is prick and cunt is cunt and soon the four of us were thrashing away like mad. I believe I nearly drowned Jack with my load even as he poured enough sperm into me to float a ship.

This change was quite refreshing to us all. A little while later both of the boys gave us another fuck and afterward we fell asleep like tired babies.

One of the girls in the freshman class with us had become very friendly with Betty and me, and we invited her to come to our apartment several times. She, in turn, had us come over to her place, which was just a room in a private house.

One night when this girl was over visiting us, Bob called up and asked us out the next Saturday night. Of course we quickly agreed.

Ethel, our new friend, wanted to know who it was, and we told her. "Oh, girls," she said, "don't go out with those boys. They are not nice. Why, Agnes and I were out with them once and we had to leave them flat in order to remain respectable."

Betty looked at me and I looked back at her. This was a new angle to us to hear a girl warning us about a boy because he tried to be nice. Most of the warnings that we had heard before were about avoiding certain boys because they were cold sticks and would not even try to fuck you. This was different.

"Do you mean," I asked her, "that if a man really wanted to love you, even just a little, that you would not allow him to do it, Ethel?"

"You bet!" she cried. "I am not going to allow every Tom, Dick, and Harry to fondle me. I have too much pride to allow that."

"Well, Ethel," I said, "I don't know what you do

for a good time, but I know that you must be missing a whole lot of fun. Honestly now, hasn't any boy ever put his finger in your little box, and haven't you ever had a fuck?"

"No, I should say not," said Ethel emphatically. "They have not and they are not going to have the chance, as far as I am concerned."

Betty and I tried to talk her into another view of the matter and even tried to get her in the bed so that we could jack her off. But she fought like a demon and threatened to report us if we did not cease. Her parents had told her that honor was to be guarded at the cost of everything. We were forced to let her go, the poor deluded girl.

We met many girls like that. There were hundreds that would not drink. But nearly all but a few liked to feel the throb of a stiff prick in their cunt at some time or other.

Time passed all too quickly, and school was over for three months. All of the boys that I had met were from other towns and cities, and, of course, Betty lived with her parents, who had moved to Washington.

That was the only lonely summer that I ever spent, and the time seemed to draw slowly by. If I had only known that the next year was to be the turning point in my life, I would have made the best of that summer. But how was I to know?

At last school opened again. Betty and I had the opportunity to choose our physical education curriculum. So we asked our guidance counselor.

We told him, quite frankly, that we had little interest in some of the physical training classes that were offered. We could see no practical aspect to swatting at some ball with a misshapen piece of wood—field hockey I believe it was called.

And volleyball? All that jumping and jumping and jumping just to punch a ball over a net. We didn't think so (though I did confide to Betty that it would be awfully fun to watch all those sweet tits and lush little bottoms hopping and flopping about).

Our counselor quickly picked up the drift of our thinking and, with a curiously knowing smile, observed, "Girls, since the school's gym facilities are overburdened every year, we have arranged special instruction off campus with Master Odani. In his youth in his homeland of Japan, he was one of his country's most promising gymnasts until a horrible accident on a vaulting horse ended his career. Now he is considered one of the finest instructors in this country. Would you like to take his course?"

Of course we did want to and were assigned to his classes. The next Tuesday we were instructed to report to the gym of Master Odani.

It looked to me like a fine apartment building from the outside when Betty and I arrived there. On going in, a little Japanese boy took our names and we were ushered into the office.

Soon a big, fine-looking Asian man came into the office and told us that he was Master Odani. He told us that he conducted a fine school and he was sure that we were going to like it. He eyed me from head to foot. I had dressed prettily and was in no way displeased at this mark of distinction on his part. He finally told me to go to Room 10, and he told Betty to go to the regular gym.

"I wish to have you examined," he explained to

me, noting my wonder at having been separated from Betty. I was game for anything and thought there may have been something to this. But I trudged alone down the hall and, coming to the door of Room 10, opened it and entered.

I was surprised that this apartment was prettily furnished and the only thing in the room that had anything to do with gym work was a long slab that looked to me like a massage table. I had plenty of time to look around and examined everything. There was a beautiful lounge with Japanese silk over it, and there were wonderful tapestries on the walls.

One thing that caught my eyes was what looked like a peephole in the wall, hidden from casual sight by the hangings. I had no sooner found this when the door suddenly opened and Master Odani and another gentleman entered the room.

I was introduced to the newcomer, Instructor Yakimoto, the head gymnast according to Master Odani. "We wish you, Miss Michelle," said Master Odani, "to undergo a physical examination. So if you will be so kind as to remove all of your clothes, we will have it over as soon as possible."

I looked at him in astonishment and he smiled and said, "Oh, that is all right, we will withdraw at once and remain out while you are being examined by the doctor." Then they both turned around and left the room, closing the door after them.

I had no reason in the world to believe that anything was wrong in this, so I at once began unbuttoning my dress and removing my clothes, placing them upon a chair at the side of the room near where I had noticed the peephole in the wall.

As I lay down my undergarments, I was sure that I saw the shutter drop. I turned about quickly as I heard the door open.

Yet another Asian entered. He closed the door tightly behind him and came to me and said, "Do not be worried, Miss. I am only the doctor. Please be so kind as to mount this examination table."

I got up on the table and lay back on it. He put his hands on my bare legs first, and then on my arms, feeling my muscles carefully.

Then his hand went down lower and rested for an instant on the silken hair between my thighs. I did not make a move. His hands went further down and then back to my breasts.

He took one of my tits in each of his hands and, squeezing them gently, said, "Most wonderful globes, Miss Michelle. You are certainly to be proud of such wonderful development."

Although I tried hard to repress it, the buttons on the tips of my tits got hard as iron and stuck out wanting to be kissed. The doctor smiled and moved his hand gently back to my most secret possession, my cunt. Only for a moment did his hand pause there, but that was long enough to set my whole body on fire with passion. Then without even a word, he left the room

I jumped up, but suddenly the door opened again and Instructor Yakimoto appeared once more. He came quickly toward me and I saw that he was now dressed in long silken robes—the Japanese native dress. He said nothing but placed his hands right on my naked breasts. I let myself fall back on the table and he, too, put his hand down to my silk grotto. As he lingered there, I felt a finger easily spread apart the hair, and felt his soft probing in my trembling vagina. Then his finger entered my cunt, and I writhed about in passion while he massaged me as I had never been stroked before.

Throwing all caution and reserve aside, I threw my arms about him and pulled him to me. As soon as he saw that I was willing to make the sacrifice, he took me into his arms and with no effort carried me to the couch that I had noticed when I first entered the room.

Placing me upon it, he loosened his robes and allowed them to fall to the floor, exposing to my gaze his beautiful naked body. However, to my surprise, he had a covering of some sort over his prick and balls.

"Come, Miss," he said, "we will have our first lesson. I am to instruct you in the art of wrestling. In order to ease our movements we have discarded all unnecessary clothing, as you see."

He again put his arms around me and picked me up. Grasping me around my bare waist, he lowered me to the floor and gently placed me upon my back. Again he picked me up and, without a word, threw me gently on the floor, where he easily pushed me on my back.

This time he was almost over me. You may believe me that I was not thinking at all of wrestling now. I was so passionate that I was almost crazy, and I would have given anything in the world to get hold of his prick, which I saw swelling under that thing he had on.

Even as he picked me up again and started to throw me on the floor, I saw my chance and I grabbed for the cloth around his waist. To my surprise it came off very easily.

His prick was longer and thinner than either Jack's or Bob's, but I had no time to ponder on this, as he again threw me on my back. I reached for his prick and deftly placed it at the entrance to my cunt, which was burning and twitching with heat. With a quick motion he jabbed it into me, and my nervous legs clasped around his muscular bottom.

For many seconds we just lay there, still, and then he picked me up and, without withdrawing his prick from my cunt, placed me on the couch and fell over me into my arms. He began to fuck me with a steady rhythm. We were engaged in the act of love when the door opened and Master Odani entered.

I was taken by surprise. Yakimoto had shot off into me. Jumping up, he took his robes and left the room without a word. I was far from satisfied and made no bones about telling the Master so. I said, "If you insist on giving girls instructions in the nude, you had also better keep us from going crazy and furnish someone to really fuck us."

"That, my dear Miss Michelle," he said, "is just what we wish to do. You and your two schoolmates were picked this afternoon as the most beautiful of the girls from the school. We have a little additional opportunity in connection with our gym. If you will trust me, I believe that I can show you something to your advantage. Please get dressed and remain with us for dinner."

I had decided for myself what I wanted to do. "Let me ask my friend to remain also," I told him, "and you may be sure that I will stay here."

"Do me the favor of waiting by this door," he said, "I will ask the little lady if she desires to take wrestling instructions. If she is anything like you, I am sure that it will be arranged." He rang a bell and told the man who answered that Miss Betty should go to his office. "You may suggest," he said, "that she take the course, but please, do not say anything else about it."

When Betty came up she was in a short gym suit, and he asked her if she would like to take wrestling instructions. Poor Betty, not knowing what it was all about, looked appealingly to me. Upon my suggestion she said, "Sure," and was told to go at once to Room 10.

After she had left, Master Odani told me to follow him, and he took me down a hall and stopped by a door. Pointing to a shutter in the wall, he said in a whisper, "Look, but do not speak."

I looked and saw Betty in the room just as I had been. I watched her strip off her gym suit. The so-called doctor made his examination. Then Yakimoto came into the room with her and they went through the same farce as they did with me. Of course, Betty reacted the same way I had. When the instructor came in, she wiggled under his fingers and almost tried to rape him, then and there.

Transfixed by the action in the room, I had not noticed that Master Odani had left my side. As Yakimoto grabbed her breasts and stuck his finger in her cunt, Betty gave a little gurgle and a sigh, and I knew that she had orgasmed.

When he lifted her to the couch and took off his robe, Betty grabbed him. Yakimoto buried his prick in her and, just as he was giving it to her, Odani interrupted them. I laughed until I almost cried at poor Betty's disappointment at not getting her oats. She was almost in tears. She made the same complaint to Master Odani when he entered, and he was pleased to see that she and I were cut from the same cloth.

It was getting late. Finally I was told to follow a servant who led me into a beautiful dining room. Odani and Yakimoto were there along with two other Asians and seven girls including Betty.

We did not have a chance to talk to each other, since a sumptuous dinner was served at once. As soon as we had finished, all of the men except Master Odani discreetly retired from the room. Then he said: "Now, girls, you have all gone through the same experience this afternoon...by that I mean the wrestling act. Each and every one of you reacted in the same way to our little farce. You showed a real liking of the things a man can give you."

At this we all looked at each other and broke into an embarrassed laughter. We were a pretty bunch if I do say it myself, and all of the girls present looked as if they were fully capable of knowing just what to do should a bare cock be pushed against their cunts.

"Now," he said, continuing, "I wish to tell you all why this was done, and what we want of you girls."

Of course at this we all sat up and listened to him with sparkling eyes. This was going to be fun.

"This house that you are in," he said, "is what is commonly called a House of Pleasure. However, we conduct this place on an entirely different scale than most. Every year we pick a few of the prettiest, nicest girls in the school about your ages and put them through the test that you girls have had this afternoon."

Of course, his talk about the prettiest and nicest girls did not fail to impress us, and we waited breathlessly for the rest of it.

"By our tests we ascertain if a girl has ever been touched and if she is of a passionate nature. Then we make our offer. You may be sure that you can do as you please about accepting it or rejecting it. If you do not care to remain with us, it is your privilege to leave. But on fear of your life do not divulge to anyone any of the scenes that you have witnessed while you were here.

"Across the street is an apartment house, connected to this building by underground tunnels. In that house we have several fine apartments, one for each of you girls. We will give you these apartments for as long as you care to occupy them. Our clientele of gentlemen is very large. Some of these gentlemen are very rich. Some are just young men out for the experience. All are known to us before we permit them to visit the apartments. We will pay all your expenses, such as clothes, toilet necessities, and so forth. As your part of the entertainment, you will receive one third of what we collect from our visitors.

"I do not ask any of you to make your answers tonight. I want you to think it over until next Tuesday, at which time you are due at the gym again. Then, if you wish to stay, we will go into further arrangements.

"If any of you feel that you were not satisfied this afternoon, that is, if you feel that that particular little spot of your person has not been properly taken care of this afternoon, I will be very glad to see that you are taken care of here, in the gym before you leave."

CHAPTER FOUR

IV

I do not know what the other girls did, but Betty and I stayed. It was not many minutes before Master Odani returned to us and told us to follow him. Addressing me, he said, "My dear, it is very much out of the regular run of things for us to enter into any of the games that are played here after the initial test. But both of you seemed so unsatisfied at this afternoon's performance, that several of the men in my employ have volunteered to attempt to give you at least a little pleasure.

"Do you two girls wish to remain together while this takes place, or would you rather be alone?"

"We'll stick together," I responded for both of us.

"Just as you please," said the Master with a smile, and opening the door of a room, he bade us enter. He closed the door behind us and I heard him lock it from his side. This scared Betty to death, but now that we were here, I was determined to get the most out the situation. I looked about the room. It was the most exquisite, most beautifully furnished room that I had ever seen in my life. Lavish drapes hung from the walls, and the furniture was all hand carved in curious designs. All of this must have cost a fortune. There were two large lounges with soft, silken, multicolored tapestries and a profusion of big pillows thrown over them. Two silk screens were placed modestly before them. Remembering the peepholes in the examining room, I looked about and, sure enough, there were more of them here. I wondered if the whole house was full of these, so that anyone could be watched at any time.

Betty, somewhat recovered from her fright, was also admiring the furniture. She came to me and, squeezing my arm, said, "Oh, Mike, I think that we have been foolish in staying here. What if all of these men make us take their pricks in us? We may be dead when it's all over. I am sorry that I stayed."

"Don't be silly," I said somewhat crossly. "I imagine you were so hot for a prick when you were in that room wrestling with Instructor Yakimoto that you didn't seem to mind who fucked you. Now that we're alone, and you don't have a man's fingers in your cunt or a stiff prick to hang onto, you are nervous. Brace up, dear Betty. In a minute or two I'm sure there will be two cocks here that will satisfy us both."

Betty had to laugh at this. She rubbed her hand between her thighs and said, "Well, Mike, I'm ready for a good fucking, and if I don't get it soon I will flood my thighs." She rubbed madly until I stopped her.

Betty and I continued admiring the furnishings and wondering how such a wonderful collection of art came to be in such a strange place when presently a door opened opposite from the door by which we had entered. In came two sturdy-looking Japanese lads whom we had not seen before.

They were both dressed in the silk robes of their native land. Both were large and good looking. Although Betty and I had both had momentary doubts about the wisdom of remaining there, there was a lot of heat and devilishness in both of our cunts. We were game enough to see something through once we had started it .

One of the lads came right over to me; the other went to Betty. Lifting us both in their arms like we were a couple of kids, they laid us gently on the two couches.

Then they put the screens in front of each couch so that neither of us could see the other. The one that had me then turned to me and let his robe fall to the floor.

I could not withhold a scream as I saw him stark naked. It was so sudden, and his dark-skinned body was glistening all over with some kind of oil. His prick was nearly twice as large as any that I had ever seen before.

He grinned at my scream. I heard an answering one from Betty and judged she was facing the same predicament. My samurai warrior lifted up the huge head of his rock-hard prick. As he presented it to me, I thought he was simply going to impale me then and there. But that showed how much I knew. That was not their method of doing business. These fellows showed they could keep their pricks hard for hours at a time while they played with a girl the way a kitten plays with a mouse—without going off in all that time.

Sitting down beside me on the couch, my samurai put his hands on my ankles and began to rub and squeeze my legs. The sensation was so good that I opened my legs and let him feel higher.

He did not get to my cunt, but felt all around it. Then, standing me up, he stripped me of my dress, leaving me my slip, bra, panties, shoes, and stockings.

Giving me a gentle push, he tipped me onto my back. He threw himself down beside me and began to fondle me all over. His playings, with his hands first on my tits, then down along my belly, and then skipping to my cunt, warmed me to him. He firmly manipulated my bottom, which he stroked and stroked, and slipping both of his hands back to the cheeks, he pulled them quickly and then released them until I could not lay still.

He had the impunity to stick the tip of his finger right up my backhole, causing me to leap from the couch. This was a new sensation for me, and it caused me to tingle from head to foot. I grew quite warm inside. Finally, as his hand again stole to my cunt and gently opened the lips and rubbed the conch-hued membranes, I gave a cry of passion. Without any effort on his part or even my being conscious of it, my hand became tightly twined around his big and throbbing prick. I squeezed and massaged it, rubbing it up and down, uncapping the purple head and feeling in my hand the giant balls that were under it and the black hair that covered his belly above it.

He thrust his belly forward at this and I, in a perfect fever of lust, pulled away at his prick as if I were thoroughly determined to pump it dry.

I cannot express how much I enjoyed the feel of his steel rod, and it gave me more pleasure to rub and squeeze his instrument than any other that I had ever held. It did not seem to give a bit under the strong pressure of my hand, except for the movement of the loose skin that covered it, which rolled back and forth. I marvelled at the staying power of this Far Eastern delight, so different from the other tools that I had known.

I could feel a throb within it and knew that the time must be near when he would bury it within me. I pumped still harder as I was all aflame with burning lust and wanted him to hurry. My quim panted and throbbed, and I spun about beneath the searching touch of his digits. He put an arm about my shoulders, pulling me close to him and hugging me so strongly that I thought that my ribs would be crushed. But it thrilled me to my very soul.

I was so carried away by emotion, so wrought up by my lustful feelings, so heated by the passionate toyings of my burnished bronze partner that I pressed my lips to his and kissed him, maddened with desire.

He kissed me back. His magnetic lips thrilled me to the very soul, and I allowed him to feel and pull me about while I frigged his prick like mad.

I knew that he could not hold back much longer and slowed down my manipulations, fearing that I might cause him to shoot without fucking me.

Ahh, at last. He threw open my thighs and put his

prong in line to drive up into me. If I had had my senses, I probably would have been terrified at the sight of this enormous machine about to impale me. But feeling as I did, the tool of an elephant would not have fazed me in the least.

Up to this time not a word had been spoken, but now my lover broke the silence with perfect English.

"Miss Michelle, do you want it?" he murmured, rubbing it against my cunt.

"Want it, want it," I panted, "give it to me, my big stud. Give me your prick right up to your balls. Fuck me. Tear me. Drive into me. Fuck and don't talk—I want your prick, your prick," and I grabbed the head of it and tried to pull him closer.

He seemed, however, to take a great delight in this teasing process. He waggled it around the entrance of my slit which was now soaking wet with my effusion. For my part, I was acting like a perfect nymphomaniac, struggling to induce him to fuck me.

He moved even closer to me. As the head of his prick found the outer entrance of my secret passage and slowly oozed within my very soul, deliciously stretching and widening my membranes, I was overcome by the most intense feelings of bliss and almost swooned while I squirmed beneath him. I poured down a charge of my dew upon the penetrating head, aiding his entrance. I soon found myself impaled upon his tool, and I danced in bliss beneath him.

I felt sure that it was all in until he lifted me in his arms. Sitting up on the couch I could see in a mirror that only a portion of his prick was in me. I pressed frantically down on it in an attempt to engulf it all. He passed his strong arm about my waist and, holding me tight, with one thrust drove it up to the balls within me. So sweet were the sensations that washed over me that I really did faint this time. I recovered to find myself again back on the couch with his huge bomber planted firmly in me to the very balls. Seeing that I had come to, he started a slow in-and-out, pistonlike motion. I fairly gurgled with joy as he thrust and withdrew his peg within my sobbing slit.

Never before had I experienced such thrilling reactions. The thought that this man was a total stranger, and a foreign one at that, made the experience that much more exciting. I bubbled and churned beneath him. Though I thought that my wild gyrations were enough to break off his iron-hard charger in my slit, he seemed only to swell larger and larger with each and every poke.

Faster and faster he moved upon me. I tried to time my jerks to his drives, feeling the apex of his passions rapidly approaching. With a few wild bounds that drove him into the hilt, he grasped me tightly in a crushing embrace. I seemed to feel the spurt and bubble of his sperm as it volleyed within me, far up into the gaping mouth of my opening. With a wild cry I fell back again, lifeless on the couch.

An echoing scream rent the air, as if in tune with mine, and in my delirium I realized that Betty, behind her screen, must be experiencing the same giddy pangs of sensual bliss that I was. As I returned to my senses, a delicious tingling and thrilling of every nerve within me attested to the soul-stirring force of the fuck.

I was surprised to feel that steel ramrod of his still

flashing back and forth inside of my body. Finally I was too weak to hold him longer, and my arms fell from about his body. Still his rapid titillations brought spasm after spasm from me. He lifted my legs, forcing them up past his body and back, until my feet were almost straight up in the air. My bottom, with its juicy cunt, was wide open, waiting to meet his savage, cruel thrusts. Then, with little squeals of delight, he came again. And what a load he poured.

This eruption brought me more burning ecstasy than I had ever known, as he spurted from his throbbing prick into my very vitals. Only one other time in my life did I feel anything like this wonderful sensation, when another geyser of hot balm was pouring into me in viscid jets…but that is another story.

After this twin charge, I was so exhausted that I was unable to rise, and lay at rest under his heavy nakedness. He, after a few more pokes and jabs, allowed his cock to flop out of me and lay panting beside me on the couch. Finally he rose and put on his robe. He gave my breasts a gentle squeeze and departed the room.

After a few minutes, Betty came flying in to me, her eyes flashing, her whole body pink and trembling with emotion.

"My god, Mike," she stuttered, "wasn't that wonderful? Why, the man must have poured a quart of his jism into me. I am soaked to the heart." She threw herself down beside me, grasped me in her arms, and kissed me warmly.

"Oh, Betty," I stuttered, "these foreign men certainly know how to pump into one."

With that the door suddenly opened and in ran two cute little boys carrying towels. They expertly washed and dried us and then left the room.

"Well, I'll say that is service," said Betty, pressing her thighs together and again rolling on the couch. "I tell you, Mike, these are strange people, but they sure know how to treat a girl."

After we had laid there a few minutes fondling each other and talking, the door opened and Master Odani came in. Smiling, he asked us if we were satisfied for the time being.

We, of course, assured him that we were and told him that if he allowed us a few more minutes of rest, we would gladly take more of the entertainment that he had to offer.

He told us that we had better run along home for now, and come back some other time. Regretfully, we got up and dressed. We made our way home, where we lay down in bed together and talked over the exciting incidents that had occurred that afternoon. We wondered where it would all lead.

Of course, we had decided to fully avail ourselves of Master Odani's kind offer to furnish us with amusement. That week we moved from our apartment to the one across from the gym.

Bob came to see us the night we moved. He asked us how it came about that we picked that ritzy place, and how the dickens we were going to afford to pay expenses.

He was acting funny. I think he knew something that he was afraid to tell us. He only told us to be careful as some of the girls living in the place had a bad name.

We were allowed plenty of time to become accustomed to our new location, and for a week we were not bothered in any way at all. We could not help hearing and seeing some things that might have caused a great deal of wonder on our part if we had not come there knowing just what to expect.

For instance, the second afternoon there, after returning from classes, we were surprised in the hall by a man who was stark naked, his long prick standing at full mast. He did not bother us at all, merely nodded recognition and entered one of the other apartments on the same floor.

We later learned that he was the only man living in the building. He was there for the same reason we were. In other words, there were some women who were hunting for the same thing that the men who were to come to us were looking for. I also found out later in life that there was a certain class of men who preferred one of their own kind at times. If they were so inclined, they too could satisfy their desires at Master Odani's.

One night, when we had been there a week, the phone rang. It was Master Odani. He told us that he was sending over two boys to meet us.

We, although desiring for a week the opportunity of entertaining some visitors, were scared to death that it might be someone we knew or that we might not do the right thing.

Hurriedly we fixed ourselves up and soon they knocked on the door. I let them in, and Betty and I breathed a sigh of relief. They were fairly good-looking fellows, so we were all set.

They were all business. After greeting us cordially

they made themselves perfectly at home. One of them immediately pulled me onto his lap, and opening his fly, pushed his prick into my hand.

I grabbed it and squeezed, and saw Betty was engaged in the same manner. Soon they had us both flat on our backs on the bed. Putting their cocks in our cunts, they banged away at us until they drowned us. It was so matter-of-fact and businesslike that I failed to derive any pleasure at all from it. I was terribly disappointed.

Bob and Jack came in later that evening. Betty and I were both so disappointed at the actions of our "customers" that we were burning up with desire. We conveyed to the boys our feelings and we all laughingly agreed to strip.

I was undressed first and, calling to Bob, I fell back on the bed. I opened my arms to him. The boy that had fucked me had done such a poor job that no sooner was Bob upon me than I whispered in his ear, "Fuck me, and fuck me good, I'm burning up."

This was the first time that I had used this word with him and he stopped a minute and looked at me in surprise. "Why, Mike, you are getting very bold," he said. "I see. Well, if you want to get fucked, I am just the person to do it." He threw off his shorts and leaped on me.

He placed his prong at my slit and with one thrust ensheathed it. He pumped away at me with delicious movements. Soon I spent down on him a charge of my passion's dew, and he spouted within me a flowing storm of his seminal charge.

This satisfied me somewhat, though I lay and begged him to leave his prick in me, enjoying to the full the last faint jerks of its head as it oozed out the last drop of his sperm.

Betty had done the same thing with Jack and had wrung the last of his come from his prick. She was lying contented in his arms.

Sure enough, after a while Bob's prick stiffened within me. I wiggled about gently and soon had it as hard as iron. I was treated to a second deluge. It soothed me like paregoric on a crying baby.

While Betty and I lay there, enjoying to the last the sweet languor that overcomes a girl when in the arms of her sweetheart, there was a faint knock on the door. I cast a terrified look at Betty and wondered who it could be.

Master Odani walked into the room, not allowing us time for further thought. Jack and Bob exchanged glances and Bob jumped to his feet, his prick sliding out of me.

"It's just as I thought, Jack," Bob exclaimed. "This son of a bitch is trying to make whores out of our girls. It is a good thing that we caught him!" Without giving Master Odani a chance to say a word in his defense, Bob knocked him down with a well-aimed blow of his fist.

Bob turned to us. "Come on, we'll help you pack your things and you can move at once to another apartment. We thought that this guy had something to do with this arrangement. We came here this evening to find out for ourselves."

Betty and I didn't say a word. We had come to the silent conclusion that fucking for pay was not at all like fucking for the plain pleasure of fucking. And, to tell the truth (as we later agreed when we compared notes in private), we were tickled to death to get away from this whole mess.

"Jack," said Bob, "you go and make arrangements to move their luggage, and we will have the girls come over to our place tonight. Tomorrow we'll help them find a place for themselves."

Betty and I spent the entire night in the arms of Bob and Jack, and many a wiggle and twist was given under the urge of their splendid pricks. The next day we rented an apartment for ourselves, right across the hall from Bob's quarters.

We had talked it over between ourselves and had decided to tell the boys the whole thing, just as it happened. When they found out the truth they insisted that we stay close to them. They would see to it that we got all of the prick we wanted.

Bob paid the rent on our apartment for a whole year and earned everything that it was possible for me to give him. After our experience as the property of Master Odani, we were perfectly willing to stick close to Bob and Jack.

CHAPTER FIVE

V

Bob and Jack eventually let us in on a big secret. There was a fraternity or club to which both of them belonged, one that was given up almost completely to sexual matters.

Bob was the president of this, and for some time he had been trying to get the rest of the members to admit girls to the meetings, but so far he had met with nothing but defeat.

It seemed that although they were all willing to go out after their meetings and to indulge in petting parties, they were dreadfully afraid to have the girls know about what took place in their rooms.

Bob wanted to know if we were both game to dress as boys, and to sneak into a meeting. We, of course, told him that we would like it very much.

It was decided that we were to be in attendance at

the next meeting, dressed as boys. Bob and Jack got us some clothes on the following day and we tried them on.

The coats were very long, hanging well below our hips, and I asked Bob why he had got them that way.

"You will wish that they were much longer," he said, "before the meeting is concluded. I will tell you right now that in the lodge room the only thing that a member can wear is his coat. So, of course, if you two girls did not have long coats, someone would be sure to see at once that you were missing a hard prick between your legs.

"Whatever you do, be sure not to give yourselves away, if you can help it. You will see everything that can be performed sexually without the help of girls—right before your eyes. Just sit still until I give the word. Now are you still game?"

We both assured him that we were, and both Betty and I got a kick out of speculating on what we were going to witness at the club.

The meeting was to be on a Tuesday night. Tuesday afternoon, on the advice of the boys, both Betty and I had our hair cut as close as we dared. As soon as supper was over, the boys helped us dress in the men's clothing, and we were all ready and eager to start out on our adventure.

The meeting was held in a lodge room. I will not give the name, but it is a place well known in Los Angeles. As we entered with Bob and Jack, we were all given keys to lockers.

As luck would have it, there were two fellows in our row of open lockers who were just getting undressed. At a sign from Bob, we stalled about for a while, watching under lowered eyelids while these fellows stripped to their skins. Then they put on their coats and went to the door.

The sight of their nakedness, their huge pricks and hanging balls, had a powerful effect on both Betty and me. I believe if it were not for the fun and amusement that we expected we would have taken a dose of the boys' sperm right then and there.

"Hurry," whispered Bob, and taking off my coat he helped me to strip; Jack did the same for Betty. After we were naked we put on the long coats. Bob and Jack did the same. We finished just in time, for just as we were leaving the door opened and three more boys came in and began to strip.

"Now don't get scared," Bob whispered to us as he guided us down the hall. Betty and I did feel funny being entirely naked except for our long coats. "The two of you just stay close to Jack. I have to take charge of the meeting. Whatever you do don't talk, or you will give yourselves away." He opened the door and the sight that was revealed would have made anyone gasp in amazement.

There were already about thirty or forty young men present. All of them were completely nude except for their coats—a funny sight to say the least. There were two rows of chairs by the wall, and I saw with relief that those who sat in the back row were shielded by those sitting in the front row. This was a good thing since Bob had forgotten that once Betty and I were seated we would expose our cunts to the gaze of anyone sitting opposite.

We could plainly see the pricks and balls of those boys who were sitting opposite the door. Luck was in our favor, and we found seats behind some of the other boys. Thus we were able to hide for the time being.

Bob went directly to the head of the room, sat on a chair that was on a platform, and at once called the meeting to order.

I will try to remember the things as they took place at that meeting, but I firmly believe that it was the strangest meeting that two girls ever had the pleasure to participate in. It's possible, due to my intense interest in the stiff pricks surrounding me that stood forth so impudently to claim my attention, that I may have missed some of the finer points of the proceedings.

As best I can remember, the first thing was that Bob rose to his feet and pounded on a little table with his gavel.

"I now declare this lodge of Free and Accepted Friggers open," he said. "Will the officers of the lodge arise and present to the chair their badges of membership?"

About eight of them stood up and, to my surprise and amazement, took their swollen pricks in their right hands and held them out before them.

"You will give five jerks for the lodge," Bob ordered, and each one jerked his prick back and forth five times rapidly.

"The officers may be seated," said Bob, pounding the gavel again.

"Will the Grand Possessor of the Royal Posterior please honor us by advancing to the Royal Pedestal?" Bob said.

We watched with amazement as one of the boys

near us arose and advanced to the front of the room and, turning his backside to the assembly, bowed to Bob. Then he turned to the members and did the same to them. Finally, turning once more, he bent over the Royal Pedestal and held his ass so we could all clearly see it.

Bob spoke again. "You will all follow your Royal Master in kissing the ass of the Grand Possessor of the Royal Posterior." Arising from his seat, he went behind the boy and kissed him right on the bare ass.

"Come on," whispered Jack. "We all have to do the same." So, following Jack in line, we pressed our lips to the boy's ass, just as everyone else did.

As the last one finished, Bob called for the Grand Possessor of the Royal Prick. This personage arose, advanced, and displayed to all in a royal fashion the very article that Betty and I were in sore need of at that moment.

Again, the same ceremony was performed, only this time, of course, it was a prick that we kissed instead of an ass.

As the last one passed and pressed his lips against the Royal Prick, Bob again rose. Placing himself beside the two in the front of the room, he announced that he would now join them in an embrace.

Then, right before our eyes, I saw the Grand Possessor of the Royal Prick place that jewel at the back entrance of the Possessor of the Royal Posterior. Slowly, without any resistance on the part of his opposite, he drove it into the Royal Asshole.

For a few minutes he worked viciously back and forth, just as if he was fucking a girl, and then, pulling it out of the other's asshole, he bowed to Bob.

It was now Bob's turn, and we watched with wide eyes as he placed the head of his prick at the boy's rear door. He soon had it within him to the balls and was wiggling his ass about. We knew from Bob's grunts that he was pumping a load into the Royal Posterior.

Bob withdrew his shriveled, gleaming prick and shaking it in his hand said, "The sacred duties of our body have now been performed as an example for you. Those of you that are suffering from suppressed heat are now at liberty to indulge yourself in a similar manner."

We then witnessed an orgy that was like nothing that I had ever even dreamed of. Almost everyone in the room was soon on the carpeted floor and, with the most unbridled lust, began to fuck away at each other.

I watched one boy, who was sitting before me, take the prick of his companion and, pulling it between his lips, begin to suck on it as if it were some nice lollipop.

Two other boys were on the floor eating away at each other's pricks. But most of the boys had their companions on their bellies and were wedging their pricks up the assholes of their passive partners.

Jack had thrown Betty to the floor. He had rolled her over onto her belly and, throwing up the tails of her coat, had placed his prick between her ass cheeks. She cried a bit as he tried to wedge it in her, but there was so much noise and groaning that no one paid any attention. Jack, lying comfortably on her, passed his hands under her belly and started pumping away while she leaped beneath him.

I had no further time to watch them, as I felt Bob—who had come off the stage—grab me and throw me to the floor. Helpless in his arms I, too, was turned on my belly and his hard prick was battering at my back door.

His prick had dipped right into my little hole and I, fearing he would split me, used all my strength to jerk myself away from it. But he pulled me back and, pushing me down with his arms, he again started.

I had no liking for this kind of play and struggled to free myself, but to no avail. I knew that it was no use reasoning with Bob, but I fought to prevent what I thought would cause me pain.

My struggle did not last long, however. I soon weakened in battling him, and he was again at me. The head of his prick opened me up and I gave a scream. I was almost paralyzed while he slowly bored into my asshole.

I thought I would die with his first thrust, but once he was within me it did not seem so bad. He thrashed away upon me and I wiggled beneath him. In some way, the feeling of his pushes seemed transferred to my cunt. A delicious feeling of bliss came over me, and I pushed back against him to allow him more play.

Bob, due to his recent bout with the Possessor of the Royal Posterior, was rather slow in shooting, but finally I felt him shower into me, his prick jerking and leaping in my rear. But the rubbing of his prick had made my ass so sore, and it grew sorer than ever with each pounding stroke. I thought that I would never willingly exchange this buggering for a thrilling fuck in the more traditional manner.

As soon as he had exploded, his juice spurting up my ass, I began to feel better. The welcome lava pouring up into my tight ass was a balm that seemed to relieve much of the pain occasioned by the heat of his thrusts.

"I hope, dear, that you are not sore at my actions," said Bob, as he led me to a chair after pulling out of my ass. "It is customary with us to fuck each other's asses, and I think you have found that it can be quite pleasant, even if one is receiving a dose for the first time."

"Oh, no," I said, "I do not mind it, Bob, it was just that I had never done it before and I thought it might hurt me.

"How did you like it?" I asked Betty who was sitting beside me.

"Oh, oh!" said Betty, laughing. "I thought for sure that when he shoved it up my ass, Jack's prick was going to tear me apart. But you can see for yourself that I am still here and kicking!"

"I do believe that you are two of the gamest girls in the world," said Bob admiringly, "and I am going to have you made members of this club right here and now!" He raised his hand for silence and explained to the amazed boys how he had conspired to have us enter the hall that night.

"And now," he said in conclusion, "these two girls wish to become members of our club. I do not think that there will be any objections to admitting them to our secrets."

"No, no!" shouted the boys. "Let them in! Let them in!" And we were welcomed by all of them.

"Shall we initiate them?" one asked. They all

agreed that, we should be initiated like the rest. At this part of my story I have an impulse to hide some of the happenings but, having promised to tell all of it, I will go ahead and do so.

As we started off, our coats were taken away, and after we had paraded up and down to allow the boys to look over our nakedness, we were led to the Possessor of the Royal Posterior. We were told to place a resounding kiss in the center of his bare cheeks. After we had blushingly complied, the Possessor of the Royal Prick presented his staff to our lips and we were forced to kiss the swollen head.

This finished, all of the boys formed lines and, holding their pricks in their hands, they ordered us to pass between them and bestow on each piston a loving caress with our lips.

This was not at all difficult for Betty and me. Many of the boys giving a forward push to their irons got them in between our lips. The delightful confusion of tastes among these throbbing organs caused us to grow hotter and hotter between our thighs.

At the conclusion of this, one of the boys presented a chamber pot to us and told us that it was necessary that we drink from the "loving cup" to pledge our allegiance to the club.

I refused and cringed when I saw it contained yellow liquid and a brown lump. But Jack, who was holding me by the arm, reassured me and told me to go ahead and drink. I put it up to my mouth and took a good long drink, although the thought of what it might have been made me feel like vomiting. As it turned out, the contents of the pot were only ginger ale with a doughnut in it.

After some talking, the boys said that the remaining act of regular initiation required that we "jack off." As all of the boys had done so when they joined the club, it was only right that we should do so also.

The mention of this brought to my mind the picture of the rubber prick that I had in my trunk. I said, "Boys, if you will put that part of it over until the very next meeting, we will both show you how girls do it by themselves, provided you will all oblige us by jacking off at the same time we do!"

"Yes!" they said enthusiastically. And it was so decided that at the next meeting we should do as I had proposed.

Everyone then participated in a free-for-all tumble about the floor. Betty and I sat watching them, getting a terrible kick out of seeing them grab for each other's pricks, sucking one another and fucking each other's asses.

This was quite a long session, and it is a wonder that we did not throw ourselves down in the midst of them and give our burning cunts to their lusty pokers. We restrained ourselves, however, knowing that if we did, Bob and Jack would be angry with us. Besides, that poking Bob had given me in the rear had taken some of the snap out of me. Watching the boys go at it made me hot as fire, but I needed a bit of a rest.

I could see by Betty's eyes that she was in the same state. She rubbed her thighs together as if she wanted to hide the lips of her twitching cunt. I reached over and touched her. She almost jumped, but she gave a little nervous laugh. I said, "Well,

Betty, how did you like your piss cocktail, to say nothing of having your ass opened by Jack?"

"Oh," she said, "that certainly startled me. But it was not as bad as I thought it might be. And as for the piss, I knew it was nothing but ginger ale all along. But, Mike, look at the prick on that fellow there!" She pointed to a big fellow who was lying on a little bit of a fellow and trying to shove a huge tool up his ass.

"I'll bet he'll never do it!" said Betty, watching with great interest. But if she had bet money she would have lost, for after a few wild plunges the big fellow got his cock in and settled down on the boy's back, weaving about him until he shot his load.

There were many sights like this going on around us. The lustful scene affected us both powerfully.

Finally the boys finished, and it was all over. The meeting was called to an end. We both went to the locker room to dress. Bob and Jack took us back home.

The boys were pleased with the way we had conducted ourselves and complimented us. Then they removed their clothes and announced that they were staying the night.

Of course, this was in no way disagreeable to us. We quickly undressed and got into bed. It was only an instant before their pricks were up to the hilt up in our cunts. Betty and I danced about under them for some time. We were all rather tired from the excitement of the evening, though, and soon, clasped in each other's arms, we fell into a sound sleep.

When we awoke the next morning, both of the boys' pricks stood up at attention. Before leaving the bed, Bob and Jack gave us both another load of their cream. Betty and I lay in bed, while they prepared to go. We talked of the happenings of the night before, and Betty giggled like a little girl when she spoke of the "loving cup."

CHAPTER SIX

VI

The following week was taken up with lessons and other school work and, having to concentrate on learning, we all managed to keep out of trouble.

Most nights after they had finished their work, Bob and Jack came to our apartment and nearly every time they slept with us. It was almost the same as being man and wife, except that we were going against convention inasmuch as we were not married and had no intentions of getting married.

During the week we had received an invitation to attend a party to be given by a rich widow at Redondo Beach. I had never had the pleasure of meeting the lady, but Betty and the boys knew her. They said her parties were amazing—everybody that attended went the full limit, and that if I went I would have lots of fun.

Of course that settled it for me. I told them that they could count on me. Soon after school Friday we were all ensconced in Bob's car, on our way to the beach.

They told us on the way out that only ten couples had been invited, that this was to be a quiet affair as far as outsiders were concerned.

The ten couples, with the hostess, her daughter and their two male friends, made a total of twenty-four people present. Finally we arrived, and I was immediately introduced to our hostess. I liked her at once.

There was plenty of liquid refreshment for all, and everyone imbibed freely. With all this drink everybody began feeling lively. Someone suggested that we have a swim before dinner and the hostess conducted us upstairs.

"The house has seven bedrooms," she said. "So some of you will have to double up. There are two double beds in each of the rooms, so it won't be so bad."

"Bob," she said turning to my companion, "you and Miss Hunt are to share my room. Jack and Betty will go with Lucille."

Lucille was our hostess's daughter. Hearing these arrangements I rather envied Jack and Betty; I thought they would have a lot of fun being in the room with Lucille.

Let me describe our hostess and her daughter. Mrs. Emry was a young-looking woman of thirty-eight. She was very beautiful, as beauty in women of that age goes. She had a full figure, not fat or fleshy, and seemed much younger than her age, which she had laughingly confessed to us.

Lucille was about our age and was admittedly very pretty. Dressed as she was in her fine clothes, which perfectly fitted her form, she would have attracted the attention of any boy she might meet.

Bob had told me that she was not married, and I was somewhat surprised to see her put Lucille and her escort, Allen, Betty and Jack all in one room. I, of course, was all eyes. I was not there to comment, however, but to enjoy myself.

Everybody was soon settled. Mrs. Emry came into the room where her sweetie was standing along with Bob and myself. She laughed and said, "Come, let's get our bathing suits. If we don't hurry we'll miss all the fun." We began taking off our clothes.

Our hostess's sweetie was not much older than Bob, about twenty-five as I judged. He was a very good-looking fellow. I believe that his name was Martin, or something like that.

Martin helped Mrs. Emry doff her clothing, and she did not seem to worry in the least that Bob and I were watching. Letting her chemise fall, she stood before us in all of her beautiful nakedness, then she stepped into the tight green bathing suit Martin held for her.

She was indeed a beautiful creature—with large firm tits, a thin waist, flaring hips, and shapely thighs—and as Martin petted and smoothed her suit about her I could not help but envy her matchless form.

But I had other things to think of. Jack was stripping my clothes off of me and soon I was as naked as Mrs. Emry had been. Looking at Martin, I saw that he was watching me avidly, his eyes lingering on my breasts and my mossy bush.

I, of course, returned the compliment and noted the size of his prick, which stood up straight against his hairy belly. Bob helped me into my suit, undressed himself, and soon we were all ready to go.

We all ran down and met the others and we romped and splashed into the water. We played and danced about, and I got many a grab on my tits and cunt. To punish the boys for this, I would seize the nearest prick and give it a squeeze in return.

Betty was getting the same treatment, and I knew by the sparkling in her eyes that she liked it. We did not stay in long, as the water was rather cold. When we tired of this play, we jumped out of the water and ran back to the house.

We all went into the big living room and warmed ourselves around the fireplace in which roaring flames licked skyward. The phonograph started and, for the first time in my life, I heard recordings of wonderfully risqué and smutty songs. They were hot and left nothing to the imagination. Our hostess told us that they were made in Mexico and then smuggled over here. They were easy to obtain if one knew how to go about it.

The boys, to say nothing of the girls, were all drinking freely. The heady effects of the liquor, combined with the suggestive songs and smutty stories from the phonograph soon had the whole bunch of us maddened with lust.

All of the boys were holding, groping and feeling the girls under their bathing suits, diving their hands into their waist and feeling their tits. I saw one of the girls tear open her companion's fly and pull out his standing prick while she pumped it before us all. As this happened, I saw Mrs. Emry nod to her pretty daughter. Lucille, who was almost drunk by now, stood up and announced that she was too hot for comfort and that she was going to take off her bathing suit to cool down.

Allen, her companion, jumped up and quickly pulled the top of the two-piece up over her head, releasing her shapely, rose-tipped globes. With shrieks of laughter, all of the boys pulled the tops off of their girl companions. They quickly stripped off their own shirts too, if they were wearing any.

Soon all of the girls in the room, with the exception of Mrs. Emry, were bare to the waist. Never before did such a tempting array of beautiful naked breasts have a more appreciative and lustful audience.

I had never seen such a collection of titties myself, each set different but lovely in its own way. As I let my gaze sweep the room, I was impressed and inspired. I stole a quick glance at my own uncovered flesh-mountains and was pleased at the sight. They were as firm and perky as any at the party, and they were tinged now with a flush of—was it pleasure or firelight?

Across the room was a blonde with perhaps the largest breasts in the room, heavy, unleashed from their restraint and slowly swaying. They were evenly tanned in their entirety, even on the underside where I would have thought the sun wouldn't reach. The blonde was naturally fair skinned but I could barely distinguish the spot where her broad nipples began, so smooth was her skin and so deep her sun coloring.

Next to her stood a thin redhead, her skin pale

and densely freckled about the shoulders and face. The cherry spots faded to pristine whiteness as my eyes focused on her lovely little mounds, high and tight on her chest. Her dark areolae stood out against the contrasting flesh. I lifted my gaze to her brown eyes, which caught mine and flashed in an instant of acknowledgement. When I looked again at her breasts, her nipples stood high and proud against a notably smaller, lighter brown background surrounded by white. She has breasts like her eyes, I thought, and I could feel my slit get moist with delight at the idea.

I looked past a number of other nubile young bodies for another contrast, another new experience, and I was stopped in my search by an olive-skinned creature of exquisite loveliness. Her form was full, her chest large, and it held its expansiveness for nearly the full length of her upper body before tapering sharply in at her waist. The breasts that adorned that broad expanse of woman were a delight to behold. I wished immediately that I could possess them, hold them and mold their firm and fleshy abundance. The fine proportion of nipple to breast thrilled me to the marrow. I wanted to take them in my hands, to finger the border between her dark flesh and the darker-still caps that graced these mounds. To flick my tongue and brush the tips of these twin peaks. To suck and nip them until they were sore with the pleasure of my desire.

For my part, I had nothing to be ashamed of in this sudden show of feminine grace. My own two orbs were on a par with the best of the girls, and my strawberry nubs stood out as though inviting the soothing caress of a male tongue.

Bob evidently thought this too, for he gathered me to him and, pressing me against his hairy chest, did that little favor for me. The other men, taking this as an example, speedily followed his act with their girl partners.

We then settled ourselves back in our seats, each girl on her boy's lap, hands where they would do the most good. The boys started telling stories that would have shocked most of us at any other time. But now, under the influence of the liquor and our nakedness, combined with the titillating touches bestowed on us by our companions, we were all laughing and giggling and listening intently to the smutty stories.

Then Lucille, looking about, noticed her mother still fully covered by her bathing suit. With a little shriek she ran over to her, grabbed the strap of the suit, and pulled it down off her mother's shoulder. She managed to pull the suit clear down to her mother's hips, and it fell to the floor leaving the beautiful Mrs. Emry stark naked before our gaze.

Gasps of delight came from the boys, and some of the girls giggled nervously. I was again spellbound with admiration for this wonderful form, so suddenly bared before our eyes.

Her bare, glistening body was a thing of delight. Rounded fully at the hips and curving well in at the front, she presented a form that would be hard to match anywhere. Her breasts were full and fresh-looking, and her beauty was without blemish of any kind. She looked about with a glance of pride and, straightening herself, held her arms high above her head in order to allow all present to study her perfect charms. Slowly she turned about, allowing us to see her beautiful dimpled posterior and wonderful arched back.

We all looked on enrapt for a moment, and then the boys applauded noisily and cried out, "That's the girl, Lucille. Brave Mrs. Emry. It is no more than right that all of the other girls follow your example."

This suggestion did not come as any shock to me, and the other girls, laughing and giggling, allowed their male companions to push down their bathing pants. I watched Lucille's suit fall to the floor, exposing her cute nest covered with a mop of curly red down to her fellow's eager gaze.

His staff rose up at the sight of it and Lucille pulled his trunks down to free it. It was one of the biggest pricks that I have ever seen. Now that she was naked, Lucille blushed rosily and turned to the protecting arms of her lover. Without thinking what she was doing, she grabbed hold of his stiff poker. Giving it a loving squeeze, she buried her flaming face in his shoulder and hid it from us.

You may imagine the effect of all of this upon the rest. The boys, also freeing themselves from their trunks, gathered us in their arms. Each girl had a prick in her hands. The boys in turn fingered each quivering cunt.

We noticed that one of the girls had shaved all of the hair off her little grotto. We all carefully examined the results of this scalping. Except for the tiniest goatee of dark hair that remained high above her slit, she was shorn clean and smooth. Between her legs, where others sported a forest, her skin was darker and her labial lips were darker still. As we all stared in wonder, this flesh portal engorged and swelled in recognition of the admiration and attention it was receiving. It fairly glowed a dark claret.

The girl grew modest after becoming the center of so much attention and tried to shrink away. "Oh, no!" cried out one of the boys, "we must see more! Spread those lovely legs and open your naked slit so we may all see the depths of your loveliness."

Emboldened by this appreciative talk, the hairless young lady sat on a nearby couch, knees pressed together, at first thoroughly blocking any view of her clean-cut slit. But then she slid forward until her fanny was only just touching the edge of the seat. Hooking her thumbs about her hips and extending her fingers down into the space between her legs, she slowly spread her legs apart, wider and wider, her painted fingernails restive beside her now-glistening, glabrous slit, accentuating its utter nakedness.

Then the crimson-tipped middle finger of each hand touched the dark outer fold of soft labia and tugged. The moist mouth of her cunt began to open and the assembly glimpsed the wet, pink inner flesh of her more intimate passage. Her index fingers joined the exploration and spread her nether lips more fully along their length, opening her still deeper to our view. The complex layers gave way to more solid structures.

Her clit stood at attention in this open field. What a study in contrasts! It was dark against the pink inner meat, all pulled into view between her red nails, the whole wonderful flesh-flower distorted by the upward pulling. Her main love canal could be glimpsed at the juncture of the V, where it oozed its sweet secretion down the bare inches of taut flesh and then trickled into the shadow and between her asscheeks, where her puckered little anus twitched provocatively.

One couple couldn't wait any longer, and flopped down on the floor and started to fuck right before us all.

Mrs. Emry, however, was not ready for that yet, and she made them stop at once. "Do not take the edge off your feelings by fucking now," she said. "There are many other things that we can do that will stimulate and satisfy our passions even more than that, but will not cool off the burning lust for more the way mere fucking will. Here. Let me show you." And taking the couple she placed them mouth-to-sex, so that the boy's prick was pointing into the willing girl's mouth, and her cunt hovered above his lips.

"Now, my children," said Mrs. Emry, "you may all watch this interesting combat, and if some of you desire to imitate the actors, just go right ahead. But remember: No fucking until I give the word."

Aflame as I already was, it was nearly impossible to restrain myself from jumping on any of the turgid tools that sprouted about me. But Mrs. Emry had been very specific, and I was willing to do my utmost to honor her request. Still, the display of oral sex that was being performed for our benefit got me wanting a wicked wand up my cooze rather than having it cooled by my willing partner's mouth.

With her back on the floor, the chosen young lady bent her knees and threw her legs back and rump up, forcing her playmate to reach between her thighs and lock his elbows about the back of her knees. As he pulled her tail higher still off the floor, exposing more of her tight beauty to the admiring crowd, his head bowed to kiss and tongue her shimmering slit.

At the other end of this love knot, the long-haired brunette beauty Mrs. Emry had selected for this taste test was enthusiastically inspecting the stiff bait that dangled temptingly above her tousled head. Throwing her arms about his legs as he held her, she drew herself up and barely touched the tip of her flickering tongue to the dripping faucet that pointed down at her. Again and again she did this, just teasing the young buck's exclamation-point of manhood, removing the moist drop that appeared at the opening of this fine pistil only to have it quickly reappear.

This repetition drove the tool's proud possessor into a frenzy of passion, and he plunged his face between her humping hips as her thighs clamped about his handsome young head. The most interesting parts of the view there were now obscured beneath the mane of his hair. Beneath that bobbing head, his mouth and nose and forehead were buried fully in her wide slit. The oral activity was ferocious: that much could be heard. But there was little visible. So I positioned myself for a better view of the other end, where his piston was now poised at the mouth of the partner whose nether openings were being devoured with such fury.

She was far more dainty in her treatment of his pulsing joystick. She puckered up and, parting her moist lips slightly, planted a slow, hot, sucking kiss upon the very tip of the inverted digit that hovered over her. This caused him to spread his legs further apart, thus closing the distance between his prick and the young lady's head as it lay on the floor.

Having lowered the proximity of his pleasure pump, raising her head allowed the cock-gobbling girl to take more of him deeper into her mouth with each subsequent kiss. Her lips moved further and further up his shaft with sucking kisses, now encompassing more of the head, then to the edge of his glans, then the whole of his mushroom cap, slurping the dripping tool as she sucked down and withdrew it from her saliva- and cream-drenched mouth.

Between these ministrations her broad tongue darted out, rolled into a little cradle and, turning at the end, traced a trail down the underside of his shaft. Then back to sucking again, taking the healthy young stud further into her mouth—and, clearly, into her throat as well, so far up his shaft did she bury her face. With each rising of her head, the tender bag of his scrotum flapped against her forehead until she reached up one of her hands and lifted it clear. With the other hand she clamped her fingers about the base of the prick pendulum and solidly and ceaselessly planted it deep in her mouth and throat and, without extracting it, sucked away in mad delight.

At the other end the favor was returned, and the tightly pressed figures rolled to their sides and continued their oral coupling for some long moments more until, satiated, they broke off to the applause of the gathered observers. He turned his smiling face, drenched with her cuntjuice, to his partner. His juices dripping from her lips, she returned the admiring glance, and the two fell into each other's arms more conventionally and resumed the osculation they had engaged in so enthusiastically just moments before.

I am not going to tell here all the other happenings of that wonderful night. There was none of us at all sober until well into the next day, and then we went at it again until Sunday afternoon.

I believe that every girl there was fucked by every man. We all had to stop and sit in a circle about the fire on Saturday night while Mrs. Emry had Lucille lie on the couch before us and spread her pretty thighs wide apart. Then, without more ado, the mother placed her rosy mouth on her daughter's pouting red lips and titillated and sucked her sensitive sheath until, with great sighs on the part of the daughter and many nervous twitches of the girl's dancing posterior, she drew forth from her a bountiful rain of love juice from those pouting lips of joy.

Many acts like this followed, and there was not a thing that was thought of that was not at once put into immediate play. It was a regular carnival of lust with the experienced Mrs. Emry in charge, and many little tricks of love were learned by all in that wonderful orgy.

I even found an opportunity to test the strength of Lucille's companion's prick, and it came about this way: While fooling about in the living room, I had passed my hand around his shaft, which was, as usual, in an erect state. Bob was busy elsewhere—in fact he was titillating the cunt of a dark Hispanic girl—and his being too involved to attend me left me somewhat peeved. I took the opportunity to teach him how to behave.

Mrs. Emry, who seemed to have her eyes everywhere, noticed this little act and nodded knowingly. She came over to me and curled my hand more tightly about the cock of the seducer of her daughter.

"Look, everyone," she said. "You will notice that Michelle, in admiration of the size of this boy's prick, has done him the honor of squeezing and compressing it for him."

At this, of course, everyone looked. Now it was too late to stop, and seeing Bob look at me with a little jealous glint in his eyes, I squeezed the prong of my companion tighter than ever.

"I think," said Mrs. Emry, laughing roguishly, "that it might be well for her to satisfy herself to the full about this thing she likes, and when she does it, it is no more than right that it should be done here." With this a chorus of agreement rang out.

I saw immediately that I was in for it. But far from disliking it, I took pleasure in the feel of this monster tool. And although I would have liked to have in privacy what I now fondled in public, I determined to make the best of what was presented to me.

Mrs. Emry bent down and whispered in my companion's ear, and he laughed merrily and looked at me. I wondered what she said, but I soon found out, as she stood up and addressed the gathering.

"Everyone," she said, "Miss Hunt has signified her willingness to take this prick and the owner has asked me to have her soothe it in a way that especially delights him. In performance of this it will be necessary for Miss Hunt to release this prong for a moment." Here she laughingly disengaged my hand, and I, not knowing what was to take place, blushed and rose to my feet.

Mrs. Emry had my companion lie on his back flat on a table, his rod standing stiff in the air. Leading me to the side of the table she pushed my hand over and I understood that I was to take his prick into my mouth and suck.

This was in no way distasteful to me, and casting another glance at Bob whose face was now lit up with the green-eyed demon of jealousy, I took the big prong in my hand and placed the head of it between my lips. Taking as much of its huge length as possible between my lips, I sucked away on it.

As I did this, I felt someone behind me, and a prick banged against my thighs. Squatting down a bit I opened them and allowed entrance to this banger, which was immediately pushed far into my cunt.

With one of these delightful prongs in my mouth and the other in my slit, I worked away like mad. I worked the muscles in my throat, trying to milk the prick that was lodged there. Then I began to bob my head up and down in time to the motion of the cock sawing between my legs. I licked up and down the shaft and swirled around the swollen crown. I lashed the very tip where the tiny slit gasped for air before taking the entire rock-hard length down my gullet once again.

At the same time, I thrust back against the pole that had been rammed into me from behind and was sliding delightfully in my pussy channel. Each time my buttocks slammed against the belly of my unseen lover, his prick banged the wall of my cavern. I must admit that I felt some small measure of pride in the way I worked those stiff tools in unison. Soon both, as though in agreement with each other, chose the exact same second to discharge, and I felt a double volley of sperm squirt into my womb and throat and almost fainted from the pleasure within me.

Finally Mrs. Emry led me gently to a couch, and to finish this double meal of prick, she opened my thighs. With the sperm still running from me, she buried her face between my thighs and sucked from me the very last drop of my essence. I thrilled and wiggled and spun about on her lips. My lust being contagious, the others threw themselves on the floor and ravished each other in all manner of forms and fashions.

This proved to be the last of our love bouts in the house of this delightful woman, and with many promises on the part of all of us to return at some later date, we regretfully left this house of pleasure and returned to our own apartments.

It took us all a week or so to get over that strenuous party. Even Jack and Bob seemed to have been well satisfied. Although they still slept with us every night, they barely penetrated us more than once a night.

Of course, Bob berated me a bit for my affair with the big-pricked boy. I retaliated with him as to his Spanish beauty and we finally agreed to forget it. Bob knew that I was crazy about prick and he was the same about cunt, and we agreed in the future to take this into consideration when out together.

The time soon rolled around for another meeting of the Free and Accepted Friggers. Bob reminded me of my promise to show the boys how the girls frigged themselves, and I told him that I would be ready and waiting to do my bit.

Betty and I were all excited the night of the meeting, and after we had got there, as soon as the meeting was called to order, I was ready. After the opening ceremonies had been concluded, Bob called the attention of the members to the necessity of having Betty and me fulfill the terms of our initiation which had been set at the last meeting.

To start it off, they helped me up onto a pedestal right in front of Bob where everyone could see what went on. I squatted down with my thighs wide apart, thus exposing fully to all of the members of the lodge a view of my already-wet cunt.

Then Betty, who acted as my assistant, handed me the rubber dildo. It had been two years since I had used it, as there were too many real pricks that needed greasing for me to waste time on a rubber one. However, the novelty of sitting before a room of thirty-five or forty boys and one other girl, and before them all frigging myself with a rubber prick, was one that would rouse the passions of anyone to a fever heat. I gave myself wholeheartedly to the operation.

In anticipation of the show I knew I would be putting on, I had trimmed my bush to allow the full assembly a clear view of the details—and to heighten my pleasure as well. As I squatted there, my buttocks brushing my heels and my knees spread wide apart, I already glistened between my legs with juicy anticipation at the delights I planned to show and share.

Supported from behind by my faithful Bob, I took the tool from Betty and raised it to my lips. Making eye contact with boy after boy—who stood before me with erections pointed at me as if they were each a compass and I the North Pole—I let each know with my eyes that the tool I now kissed and licked was, in my mind, his tool. My nipples got hard at the thought, and the boys cheered at the evidence of my rising passion. Blood rushed to the darker, slickly shaved skin at my centerpoint and, to my amazement, I came then and there without having even touched myself. This was going to be fun!

Sopping wet at my cunthole, I took the manlike shaft in both my hands and lowered it slowly down my front centerline, nestling it briefly between my breasts and bowing my head to suck and kiss it in that position. Then, moving the tip of the weapon from nipple to nipple, I prodded them back into enthusiastic erection as they had dilated into broader circles following my initial outpouring of passion. Afire again, I moved the dildo lower in the process of squeezing my tits together between my upper arms and causing them to protrude dramatically.

The prick, head up and shank down, was now at the patch of hair I had not shaved away above my steamy slit. I changed its angle until it stood horizontal to my body, butt end to me, and I waggled the weathercock at the boys as their tools pointed at me. With a cheer they, to the man, grabbed their tools and waggled them back at me, some of the fellows shooting off in the process.

Then I completed the rotation of the hard rubber prick, pointing it down at my waiting slit. I rubbed its head on my little patch of down, then touched it just below my mons at the bared opening of my pleasure gate. Pressing it to me, beneath my fleshy outer folds, I touched my trembling little counterpart with the hefty fellow I grasped in my hand. Supported by Bob and Betty from behind so as to not block the view, I dropped my other hand and spread my outer labia to afford eventual entrance to the shaft. But that act was not yet in my plan.

Spreading my legs as far apart as I could, I fingered myself more deeply and spread open the next layer of fleshy folds so the boys could have a clear look at all my finer parts. I kept the rubber prick poised above my now-exposed pink love button, and I'm sure the contrast made a charming sight. Taking my drenched clit between my fingers, I stroked and teased it until I shuddered once again in a fit of passion. This was more fun than I had anticipated in my wildest imaginings.

Now I was really ready to penetrate myself for the boys. They were ready too, it was clear. I slid the downward-pointing dildo forward along the length of my slit, letting my cunt lips wrap about it and using the tip to ravage the hindmost part of my opening, a place of particular pleasure for me. With the prick sliding and slurping along my clean-shaven, rubbed-red twat, I raised my free hand, soaked with my juices, to my breasts, then to my lips. Tossing my head back, I plunged my sticky fingers into my mouth and sucked and sucked as my other hand worked the dildo all about my slit and at the opening of my deepest passage.

Now I needed a prick far up in me. While I would rather have accommodated any of the real flesh spewing about in front of me, a bargain was a bargain, and I moved to finish the act with my old friend the rubber dildo. Keeping the head at the opening of my box, I held it erect there for some long moments, poised above it, barely spread by it, touched by passion for all the boys to see. Then they began to softly chant, "Take it, take it, take it." And the speed and the volume gathered momentum like an approaching freight train. I picked up the pace of their chant and squatted down hard, then lifted, then took the dildo hard and fully in me again as they kept the cadence, "Take it, take it, take it."

Then one corner took up the cry of, "Deeper, deeper, deeper," and soon all took up the call as I pounded the prick harder, faster, deeper into my flaming opening. I was dizzy with the speed, the heat, the excitement of it all. The boys were generous in their enthusiasm.

I writhed and tossed on the pedestal and would have surely fallen off it had it not been for stalwart Bob, who held me tightly from behind. I kept on working the prick back and forth within me, faster and faster until, with thrills and moans of delight, I poured forth my foaming tribute.

It was now Betty's turn, and with pretty grace she mounted the pedestal. Daintily opening her thighs, she allowed them all to look at her while she placed the prick within her and spun about on it till she finally vented. This act so affected the boys that most of them could not resist the temptation to keep up with her. The sight of all of those boys jacking off in front of us again brought back my strength, and I was soon as passionate as I ever was before.

The rest of the evening, like that of the previous meeting, was spent in general fucking. In accord with the talk that I had with Bob before we came, I allowed any of the boys that wished it to fuck me. Betty did likewise, and I do not believe that there were any of them there that did not want to take a shot at us, judging from the number of stiff pricks that were presented for our attention.

At any rate, it is unnecessary for me to say that, for once, we were both well satisfied as to prick. Not only our cunts but our assholes and mouths received the tender consideration of the boys, and the next day both my cunt and my asshole were so sore that I was in actual pain.

That was the last party that Betty and I attended while at school. The very next day Betty got a wire that her mother had passed away and she was to come home at once, so after kissing Jack and me, and not forgetting Bob, she left that night.

CHAPTER SEVEN

VII

The next week the boys had to go to Portland with the track team and I was left comparatively alone. Used as I was to the companionship of my three friends, this Saturday seemed to be the longest one that I had ever known, until late in the afternoon. Then an incident happened which will show to what extent I would now go in order to satisfy my passions.

The man and woman that owned the apartment where I resided did not live in Los Angeles. However, they had come for a visit and were stopping while they were in the city.

They were fine people and did not have any idea of the terrible extremes to which I and my companions would go to derive sexual amusement—naturally, not knowing anything about our conduct, as we kept that secret from everyone except the participants.

They had a daughter my age, perhaps a bit younger. But no matter; she appeared even younger still, almost childlike in her nominal pubescence and likewise quite immature in her behavior. The day of their visit, of all days, they wished to go somewhere without taking this woman-child along with them.

Seeing me at home, they asked me if I would do them the favor of keeping company with her the next day while they were away. Of course, I could not very well refuse to perform this favor for them; I was not going out and indeed had no reason to do so.

At that time, however, I had no idea of doing what I really did do. The events of that afternoon were entirely unpremeditated.

Marjorie—that was the visitor's name—came up a little later, and after looking around told me that she was going to sit out in front of the house.

An hour or two later I decided to get dressed, as it was possible that some of the boys from the club might call and ask me to go to a show or something, and in case that happened I wanted to be ready so that there would be no reason for me to miss a good time in their company and maybe a fuck.

I took a bath and had just slipped on a silk teddy when Marjorie came running into the room. As she saw me, clad only in my teddy, she suddenly stopped and looked at me spellbound.

She was a pretty little elf, and as she stood there looking at me, the memory of my younger days came back to me in a rush. I wondered about her experiences and suspected they were nonexistent. I wondered, too, if she longed to be shown the mysteries of sex as I myself had so long ago.

"My, how beautiful you are, Michelle," she cried with her eyes still fixed on my person. "Please, do you mind if I look at you? I have never—never seen so beautiful a person, and I—I—may I touch you?"

The unprompted desire of this sexual novice to caress me, to explore me, to call me beautiful as she did, had a powerful effect upon my feelings, you may be sure. With my mind in a perfect tumult of emotions, I of course told her yes, that she could, as yet not knowing that the soft touches of her body would inflame me beyond control.

When I finally knew, it was too late, and then I did not want to turn back. And to tell the truth, I do not think that precocious little Marjorie wanted to either.

With a cry of delight, I took the girl into my arms and held her tight for a moment. Then, releasing her, I kissed her again and again, reveling in the tremulous feel of her rosebud lips.

Finally she looked me full in the face and said, "Why, Michelle, no one has ever before kissed me like that. I like it and I am sure that you are so sweet and so lovely that I love you."

Almost without knowing what I was doing, I took her on my lap and began to gently stoke her. I boldly laid one of my hands on her leg and, squeezing and molding it, I slowly raised it higher and higher and she held me close.

"Do you like that?" I asked her, still squeezing and patting her youthful limb.

"Oh, yes," she said, "it feels very nice, and you are so beautiful!"

Pressing her to my breasts, with the top of my

naked body of a young Venus you have yet much to live for. You have indeed missed a great treat.

Thrill after thrill went over me as I examined charm after charm while I slowly unclothed her. Finally she stood naked as day before me.

Disregarding her lack of experience for a woman of her age—nearly the same as mine, I had concluded—her body appeared hardly pubescent. She was developed proportionately and attractively, just not greatly. Her breasts were swollen lumps on her chest, not heavy with maturity but ripe with the promise of endowment. They made me think of a vanilla sundae—two dips of milky white ice cream, each crowned by a red cherry.

The muscles beneath her skin were soft and supple but lacked definition, although she was shapely and well formed in her way. She was slim and nearly boyish to my eyes, with ribs showing through beneath those tasty little breasts and a bit gangly in her limbs, though attractive enough in an unsophisticated sort of way.

And her love-pocket! Now that was a sight. Although fully furred, her slit and all the details of her female anatomy were visible through the mist of fine, golden down that glistened in the sunlight and fired my passion anew.

"Now take off that pretty thing," she said, pointing to my teddy, and I lingeringly let it slip from my shoulders until I was as naked as she.

"What nice hair you have there," she murmured. "Isn't it just wonderful? It's so soft and nice!" And she grasped a tendril of my pubic hair and twined it in her tiny fingers causing thrill after thrill of sensual pleasure to overcome me as she made a careful search and examination of my parts.

"Yes, dear," I said somewhat faintly as she gently pulled my hair. "That's what we call our pussy. Do you like to play with it, Marjorie? Look here, this is its mouth!" And I put my hand down and pulled the lips apart, allowing her to look within the hot confines of my slit.

"Oh," she said, stooping down to see this wonderful thing more fully. "It's all pink—and wet! It looks nice!"

"Nice enough to kiss?" I asked her. "If you really mean that, would you kiss it and prove it to me?"

In answer to this she pressed her lips to me, and for a moment I thought I would surely swoon away, such was the delight that she gave me with the contact of her lips on my burning quim.

That soft little face of hers was so beautiful and childish, and she seemed so interested and so lovable. I knew that all this now taking place with her was a new and wonderful world that was being opened to her untutored mind.

Such a slight little waif she was that I easily turned her and managed by bending a lot to reach her cunt with my lips. I placed a kiss upon her pussy, but it was impossible for me to suck her while her lips were on my slit, so thrilling was the feeling that she inspired within me.

Finally, just as I felt the ecstasies of pleasure overcoming me and I was about to come, there was an insistent knocking at the door.

A thousand feelings overcame me, but I was so hot that I did not care who or what it was. Quickly arising and donning a robe and a demure expression, I went and opened the door to find it was only a messenger boy with a telegraph.

This was a great relief to me. While I was hastily signing for it, he asked me if there would be an answer. This made me look at him, and I noticed that he was barely of age himself, and not bad looking as boys of his type go. Without thinking—the telegram's arrival had so startled me—I asked him to step in while I read the message. Turning around, I saw Marjorie still on the couch, naked as I had left her, and the boy looking and grinning in a wise way.

I judged that it was now too late to do anything, and opening the telegram I found that it was an innocuous invitation from dear Betty to go to her and spend the summer with her and her father.

After reading it I lifted my eyes to the boy and I saw that his eyes were still riveted upon Marjorie's nakedness, and that the girl did not seem to mind it in the least.

Then an idea came to me. Why not give this little woman-child who seemed so willing to learn the sweet pleasures of love her first taste of prick?

Could I do it? I was pretty sure, from the grin on the messenger's face, that he'd be a willing accomplice, and not at all opposed to spending a while in our company. Turning to him, I asked, "What is your name?"

"Jerry," he said, his eyes still on my young companion.

"Well, Jerry, I see that you are all eyes for my girlfriend here, and I just wondered if it would be possible that you could stay a while. If you do so, you may be sure that it may prove, well, interesting to you. What do you say?"

"Sure, lady," he said. "I'm in. As far as I'm concerned, I could stay here forever."

"Ah. That's it, then," I said, gratified that I had not been mistaken in my judgment. I locked the door behind him, then went back to the couch and, drawing him onto my knees, let my robe fall open. As I passed my arms around his neck, I pressed a sensual kiss on his willing lips.

He returned it with vigor and, reaching over one of his hands, he thrust a finger up Marjorie's cunt and wiggled it about. I allowed my hand to fall to the front of his pants and, opening the buttons, pulled out his prick—which of course was stiff and standing. I had expected less, and was agreeably surprised at the length of it. As I rubbed it up and down, it leaped and throbbed under my touch. By now Marjorie, to see better, had sat up and was looking at it.

"Oh," she said, "what a big thing he has, Michelle! That is not at all like yours or mine."

"No, Marjorie," I said, "that is a boy's tool, and it is called a prick, and if you are good I will let you see more of it. But for the present, I think that it will be best if Jerry rids himself of all of these clothes which hamper a view that I am sure will prove interesting to you." Then, pulling the boy to his feet, I unbuttoned all his clothes and soon he was as naked as we were.

He almost gurgled with delight at this and, taking him again on my lap, I played with his prick. He, diving one of his hands down between my thighs, stuck one of his fingers in my cunt and, searching out my fancy-button, soon had me kissing and hugging him as if I were about to come.

This was too much for me alone, so I bent over and took the head of his prick in my mouth. Sucking his prong and balls, I soon had him harder than ever. Then I pushed him off me and, lying on the floor, I opened my thighs and pulled him over me. Marjorie was an interested spectator of all this but said nothing, merely watching us. I took the head of his prick and placed it within the lips of my slit and, giving an upward thrust, impaled myself upon it.

Oh, what bliss overcame me at the touch of that hard stick! I wove and threaded beneath it, and no sooner was he within me than my honey pot commenced to clench and unclench it almost peristaltically.

By this time Marjorie was on the floor with her face almost onto our parts in order to notice all that transpired. The little fellow bravely bore away into me, while I writhed about like a worm on a pin and, with closed eyes and gritted teeth, tried to break his back with pleasure.

The knowledge that I had within me the prick of an inexperienced lad, however large in size, gave added zest to my lust. He seemed to enjoy it as much as I did.

I must have exploded at least four or five times. As for him, I do not know to this day whether he shot his load or not, for I feared I'd tire him, and realizing that my time was limited, I allowed him to withdraw. Panting, I rose to my feet.

His prick seemed just as hard as ever, soaked as it was now with my generous effusions, and I carefully wiped it off with a silk handkerchief and then applied a towel to my own inflamed parts.

Marjorie had been an eager spectator to all of this lovely play and her eyes were as big as saucers. Making her again lie on the couch, I drew the naked boy to me and, taking him on my lap, again fondled and played with his stiffened rod.

He in turn kissed and caressed me warmly. I was agreeably surprised at such knowledge in one so young, so I said, "Why, Jerry! You seem to know all about handling the girls. Can it be that you have been through this before?"

"Oh, yes!" was the astonishing reply. "I have had several good fucks before this, and I like it a great deal." Then he grasped my tit and, placing his lips to the nipple, sucked on it as if to draw my very soul from me.

"Your neighborhood girlfriends, I suppose?" I said, anxious to have him recite the details in order to heat up my imagination.

"Oh, no," he said, momentarily removing his lips to answer me. "It was women—grown women like yourself—that I did it to. Why, one of them lives only a block away from here, and nearly every week or so we get a call at the office from her and she always asks that I be sent, as she knows my number and tells the manager who answers the phone that she wants me because I have such a good memory when she sends me on errands."

I mentally made a note that, in the future, when I needed a hurried bit of poking I only had to step to the phone. Begging Jerry to relate his pleasant adventures with this woman, I took hold of his stiffened prick and frigged it slowly up and down while he regaled us with a description of his fair paramour and seducer.

It seemed she was a woman of means, as she always gave Jerry a few dollars for himself. He thought that she was married, as she wore a wedding ring. Of course this might mean nothing, but she had had Jerry come a number of times. The boy was always anxious and eager to answer her calls, especially when he had "hot nuts," as he put it.

I had never heard Bob, Jack, or any of the other boys use this expression, and I filed it away as a surprise for them. After Jerry had detailed to me all of the actions and the charms of his generous companion, I again felt my blood coursing warmly within me and resolved to finish what I had in mind when I first induced the boy to stay with us: namely, the seduction of Marjorie.

"Jerry," I said, "I see that you are casting your eyes at my virginal little friend there. Do you think, if I let you, that you would be able to fuck her—and make it a good rousing fuck while you're about it?"

He grinned at this and drew away from me as if he would like to start at once. But I restrained him and laughingly told him not to be so impatient.

"No, Jerry," I said. "You must be more of a gentleman in the act, as I am not sure as to whether she will be able to take within her that great hard prick of yours. It is such a surprising size for one of your stature!

"Come here, Marjorie," I said, drawing her to me. And as Marjorie obediently drew near, I took her hand and placed it about Jerry's prick. She squeezed it tightly as she had seen me do.

This was quite agreeable to Master Jerry, who drew her to him and kissed her. I, taking advantage of their actions, slipped a finger up the girl's cunt. I was agreeably surprised and relieved to find that my finger slid entirely within her: She did not seem to possess a maidenhead. This removed all danger of her being injured and, knowing this, I proceeded immediately to the task at hand.

I placed her flat on her back on the floor, and when Jerry moved over her, I introduced the tip of his hard prick into her slit. Shoving away, he soon had it buried to the hilt within her. He passed his arms about her loins, pulled her little ass to him, and started fucking away with beautiful long, deep strokes. Marjorie said never a word, but held her lips to his like any lover. I thrilled to the sight of these two youngsters dashing madly away in that sweet embrace that brings heaven to the senses.

Marjorie opened her eyes, and I saw that they were bright as stars from the pleasure induced within her by the boy's standing cock. He, his jabs growing a little speedier, caused her to wiggle beneath him, and I knew she was experiencing the thrills of feminine passion for the first time.

A sudden shivering of his form, a rolling of his eyes, and a few gasping drives told me that he was shooting within her. Losing all control, I threw myself on the bodies of the pair and wiggled about in transports of passion.

In a few moments I arose, allowing Jerry to arise and helping Marjorie to her feet. She was surprised and relieved to find that she had not suffered in the least from Jerry's assaults upon her.

She had not even bled, but the lips of her slit were red and inflamed from the rubbing of the boy's tool. A slight stream of cream oozed out of her, which I greedily licked up. Jerry, watching me with that silly grin on his face that some men wear afterwards, shook his prick up and down at me. To my surprise, it had apparently lost none of its former hardness.

Resolving to reduce it to a state of floppy subjugation, I returned to him and, placing the head of his prong within my lips, sucked and tongued it so furiously that in a bare few minutes he spurted into my mouth. When I'd drawn the last gallant drop from him, we sank back upon the couch.

This concluded our little debauch, and after warning them both not to speak a syllable to anyone concerning the pleasures we had enjoyed, I helped them both to dress. After giving Jerry a substantial tip—turnabout is fair play!—I opened the door and, seeing no one about, allowed him to leave.

The school year being over, I soon left for the estate of Betty and her father.

Upon arriving, I quickly developed an intimate relationship with that fine gentleman, one that through the years became as important to me as my caring relationship with his beautiful daughter. And he, in his wealth and comfort, made every effort to see that we wanted for nothing.

You will recall, of course, that it was he who had presented Betty with the marvelous dildo that began our adventures in pleasure together. It turned out that he himself was the model for the tool, and the years since its creation had not dimmed his size or capacity to give a girl a really fine fuck.

Many idyllic evenings and sun-drenched morning awakenings were spent with him raptly insisting on hearing the tales of our exploits. While our limited experience meant our supply of stories was soon exhausted, Betty's father had, it seemed, a boundless repertoire. It soon became our fashion, following dinner, to take coffee or a brandy in the library or on the patio overlooking the grounds. There he would regale us with one of the tales of his experiences, or the sexual trials and tribulations of one of his acquaintances.

These episodes nearly always began in the most decorous and civilized manner and virtually always ended in a debauched romp with the master of the estate, so inspirational were the tales and the telling. He was a regular Scheherazade of titillation.

He had more than a thousand and one experiences to share and could weave them seamlessly into a narrative that quickly set my twat twitching and itching for a hearty rogering. Needless to say, Betty or her dad—or Betty and her dad, for that was the kind of caring, sharing family they were—regularly helped scratch that itch, as I did for them.

If you have enjoyed my tale up to now, perhaps you'll enjoy some of the tales with which we were regaled by Betty's father. I'll put down several of my favorites here for your edification. Let me say that I hope they do as much for you as they did for Betty, her father, and me.

CHAPTER EIGHT

VIII

DIARY

(a tale as told by Betty's father)

As I was walking along the streets, I picked up a small, leatherbound book. Looking inside, I found that it was a diary, upon the flyleaf of which was inscribed the name and address of Daisy Collinsworth. I thrust it into my pocket thinking to return it the next day.

That evening I recalled the diary and, taking it from my coat, I lay on the bed and commenced looking through it. Glancing here and there I saw nothing of interest and was about to lay it aside when my eyes caught a sentence which aroused my curiosity. I at once turned toward the beginning of this particular entry.

I was well rewarded as you shall see when you read the following, which I have copied just as it came from Daisy's pen:

Dear old Diary:

I have neglected you most shamefully for the past few days, but then, dear diary, I have had ample reason to do so. So many exciting events have taken place, such wonderful, thrilling things, that I do not know how to start telling you.

It all began with my finding a letter, addressed to Anne, our cook and maid. Quite by accident I came upon the letter in the hall, and was much astonished to learn that she had a lover. The letter was from him and read, as near as I can remember, about like this. "Dear Anne, life of my life, heart of my heart, I love you. It seems ages since we last met, since I glanced into your adorable and darling eyes that twinkle like the stars. Ah, sweetheart, can it be only one week since I had that happiness? No, it seems ages, millions of years, billions of minutes, which have dragged themselves with leaden feet across the dull, prosaic horizon. Ah, but then, my love, lean out of the latticed window tonight when everything is ready, for I shall be there, and I faint with desire to hold you once again in my arms. I will make up for the lost moments, and ages of bliss shall be ours. We will be alone in your room as before and, darling, I long to wrap my arms around your sweet body and crush it to mine. Tonight, my love! Hasten those leaden hours till night draws her sable robe about us both and bids me come to thee. Yours, with love."

This letter filled me with a curiosity not at all in keeping with my station in life. In all my eighteen years I had never been with a member of the masculine sex but had often surmised that it must be quite pleasant to have a lover.

The reading of this flaming epistle seemed to set all my senses tingling, and burning flushes shot all over my body. I thought of taking the letter to Anne and making her tell me all about it, but at last I decided to hide myself in her room and see for myself just what would occur. Anne might not relish the idea of the letter having been read by me, and to inform her might spoil the party for both of us.

Anne's room was located over the kitchen and the stairway from the kitchen had a door leading directly into the upper hallway. This door was kept locked, but I knew where the key was to be found. That night after the family had retired, I slipped out of my room and tiptoed down to and entered the room adjoining Anne's. Through the wall I could hear Anne. It was a warm and sultry night, and I wore only a chemise.

On the stroke of eleven, I heard Anne open her window, and shortly after leave the room very quietly. In a moment I was at her door and, slipping into her chamber, I concealed myself in the corner behind the curtains where Anne kept some of her clothes. While I could not be seen unless someone pulled the curtains aside, I had a full view of the entire room, which was lighted by a large lamp.

My heart was beating rapidly and I was shivering with excitement as I wondered what I would see. I was not long kept in suspense. Soon I heard a voice, softly whispering, and footsteps on the back stairs. Presently Anne came in, followed by a youth of about twenty-five. He was rather small but extremely good looking, with lovely dark hair and dark flashing eyes. Although slender, he looked strong and muscular. As soon as Anne had locked the door, she turned and clasped her arms about his neck. He hugged her to him in a most affectionate manner. They exchanged a volley of hot, passionate kisses. Then sitting down on a chair, he pulled her to his lap and began to caress and fondle her. She returned his voluptuous kisses in a distracting way. During this exchange of kisses and caresses they murmured tender words of love.

Anne is easy to look at, being about twenty-two, lithe and solid, weighing perhaps 120 pounds, and finely shaped. She has light brown eyes, golden brown hair, and cherry lips, just made for kissing. Arn (to give him the name signed on the note) seemed to be of a most ardent nature as he pressed hot kisses on her mouth. Leaving her lips after a while, he proceeded to plant kisses upon her neck, descending to her lovely tits which he uncovered in their entirety.

She was half reclining, with one hand on his shoulder and the other arm about his neck. He held her to him with an arm about her waist while with the free hand he molded her boobs; her lips were parted and from her short, rapid breathing she seemed to be greatly thrilled. Her breasts heaved and her face took on a deeper flush.

Leaving her breasts, he reached down and began to fondle the plump calf of her leg, pushing her dress up as he gradually approached her knee. Reaching this objective, he toyed with her garter and stroked her leg, occasionally permitting his hand to stray beyond the confines of the garter. As he attempted to explore still further, she stopped him with an impetuous gesture.

"Oh, Arn, dear, don't go any higher now; wait till we get into bed. It might be disastrous."

"All right, darling, but let's hurry, for I have a week's savings to invest."

Anne jumped off his lap, saying, "I am just as anxious as you to spend my savings, but you must unlace my boots." She stood in front of him and placed one foot on his knee.

Reaching down, he unlaced the shoe and then, before she could remove her foot, he had unfastened the garter and turned down the silken stocking which he stripped off her leg. Fondling the soft curves as he did so, he quickly removed the other shoe and stocking, after which he stood up and began to unhook her dress. He did not stop there but assisted her to remove all her garments, only pausing momentarily to fondle each new attraction as it was exposed to view. She was soon standing before him completely nude.

As he reached for her she coyly slipped aside. "No, no! Not yet! Don't be impatient. Wait till you are undressed. Never keep your clothes on in the presence of an undraped lady!"

He laughed good-naturedly and hurriedly undressed with her assistance. As the shirt was pulled off over his head, Anne was standing between him and my hiding place, completely shielding my view of that which my aroused curiosity desired most to see. Then she retreated to the bed, and there was exposed to my gaze for the first time the naked form of a man. I, who had never seen even a boy's juvenile toy, and whose only knowledge of the difference in sexes had been gained from other girls' tales, now had before me a grown man's sexual organ in all its pristine vigor.

His cock was standing out straight, seeming to sprout out below his belly from a thicket of hair. To my maiden eyes, it seemed of immense size. I was trembling with eagerness, an excitement which caused a strange longing to come over me. The blood coursed through my veins and I could scarcely restrain myself to stand there, an inactive spectator to the pleasure now evidenced by the lovers. I trembled and sighed and longed to rush out from my hiding place and brush Anne aside while I claimed the right to toy and fondle with this intriguing cock. My cunt felt moist and warm. It itched and ached to feel the thrill of that upstanding staff. Feverishly my hand went under my chemise, seeking and finding a throbbing spot. My breasts heaved and palpitated. I, a virgin, was about to see consummated that wonderful act of sexual intercourse.

Knowing that I had not the slightest right to be there, and the added sensation of enjoying a feast even by proxy, my pleasure was doubled. It was with great difficulty that I held myself to the role of spectator. The desire to leave my place of concealment and participate in what was to follow was almost overwhelming.

Anne lost no time in taking her position on the bed. Placing herself on her back, she separated her legs invitingly and extended her arms to receive her lover. To a man just about to indulge in the glorious rites of love, she must have presented an enticing picture, for Arn, despite his evident impatience, stood at the foot of the bed some moments, gazing in rapture at the wealth of feminine charms so generously exposed.

His position was near me and we could both gaze upon the full, round hips, the white skin of her stomach, and her firm, pointed breasts. The red lips of her cleft showed between her spread legs under a cluster of light brown curls. I was so close that I could have reached out my hand and touched her. I stooped down to bring my eyes to the level of the bed, the more closely to observe their motions.

As he laid down upon her, Anne reached over and clasped one arm about Arn's waist, drawing him to her, while with the other she grasped his rigid staff and gently began to rub the rosy tip against the lips of her cunt. Leaning over, he endeavored impatiently to force it between the moist lips, in which movement she gently tantalized him by withdrawing her cunt from his reach. After several moments of this teasing, she pointed the head of his prick against the warm lips and he responded with a furious thrust which gained the entrance. She then raised her legs and wrapped them around his back, beginning at the same time to wriggle and twist, thus drawing him down as she heaved forward. I was amazed to see that she had driven the entire length of his immense cock into her cunt, and that their belly hair was mingled.

Now they began to work in unison, a come-and-go movement, wriggling and twisting their bottoms violently while long, loud sighs of pleasure testified to their enjoyment.

"Oh, this is wonderful after being deprived so long. Oh, darling, isn't love grand, sublime, marvelous? Oh, I shall expire with the pleasure!" gasped Anne.

Soon Arn increased his furious thrusts. Faster and faster his glistening shaft glided in and out of her cunt, which clung to it as if afraid to lose it. I could hardly follow the motions as it rapidly plunged in and out so smoothly. The bed shook and creaked in the excitement of their exertions. Suddenly, uttering a low cry of delight, they seemed to blend in one fierce effort. They held their bodies stiff for a moment, then there was a lunge and thrust that defies description. They seemed to pause in a moment of ecstatic bliss while their bodies quivered and trembled in the zenith of lust and sensual delight. In another moment they were sinking exhausted in each other's arms and I perceived a whitish fluid trickling around the lips of her cunt and dripping from his cock.

The voluptuous scene filled me with an indescribable desire. I was wild with passion. Carried away with my emotions I had rubbed my thighs together, but this had only made it worse. The burning heat in my cleft filled me with a wantonness and longing for immediate relief. I felt that I would die if I didn't get it. Unless I could enjoy the delights I had just witnessed, life would not be worth living. My agitation was such that I completely forgot my situation and poked my head through the opening between the curtains. Recollecting my position I hastily withdrew it, but I must have made a noise for Anne exclaimed, "Oh, Arn, there is someone behind that curtain!"

He sprang up in surprise, ran to my hiding place,

and grasping me by the arm, dragged me into the light. Adding to my confusion and embarrassment was the fact that I wore only my chemise, and he was completely naked.

"Who the hell are you?" he managed to gasp as he looked me over.

My discovery had come so quickly that I was unable to speak.

"Oh!" cried Anne, leaping up in astonishment, "My word! It's Daisy. What are you doing in my room?"

I had recovered some of my composure and, knowing that I had the best of the situation, replied with clearness, "Well, Anne, I found your note and, learning that your lover would be here tonight, I just thought I would see for myself how you employed your spare time."

Anne immediately flared up and exclaimed, "Well, young lady, I hope you are completely satisfied with your detestable spying. I suppose you will now gallop off and tell your folks all about it, and I shall be discharged. But I don't care. I know where I can get another job." Then, turning to Arn, she continued, "I guess, my boy, we had better get out of here before this little bitch sets up an uproar and alarms the entire household."

"Hold on! Wait a minute! Not so fast, if you please! It's an obvious fact that I spied upon you, that's admitted. But listen to me: It was not done with the intention of getting anyone into trouble."

"No?" responded Anne in a decidedly hostile tone.

"Indeed not. I merely wanted to satisfy my curiosity as to how people make love, and really, the exhibition was an eyeful."

"So you had your wish granted and you liked the exhibition, eh?" said Arn, laughing.

"Well, it seemed all right from the viewpoint of a spectator, though I believe a personal demonstration would have had a better effect," I replied.

"Well now, if Anne thinks she can spare a little of my time, I believe I can demonstrate to your satisfaction. How about it, Anne? Shall I attempt to relieve this young lady's pains, for her face tells me she is in agony."

"All right. Maybe you've got enough for both of us," answered Anne, yielding more or less gracefully. "Here, let me remove that chemise." And so saying, she deftly lowered the garment and slipped it from under my feet as Arn picked me up and carried me to the bed. Lying down beside me, he began at once to press hot kisses on my lips, at the same time opening my thighs with his hand. Placing his head over my breasts, he kissed and sucked my nipples. Taking my hand, he placed it on his fallen cock which I noticed was already showing signs of renewed life. An exploring hand found my throbbing cunt. His caresses, the contact of our naked bodies, and above all, a magnetic thrill that played through me as his skillful fingers tickled my cleft, filled me anew with overwhelming desire, the like of which I had never felt before, and beyond the power of words to describe. Eagerly caressing his tool, and running my fingers through the crisp hair, I was filled with inexpressible joy as I felt his member swelling under my fingers. Arn slipped a finger into my cunt and I was fairly beside myself with the delicious sensation.

Finally, when I was almost fainting with desire, he raised me up and asked Anne to place a pillow under my hips. He then threw himself between my open thighs, clasping his arms around my waist. This brought the throbbing head of his prick against the lips of my burning cunt. Anne, getting behind us, took his prick in one hand and opened the lips of my cunt with the other, bringing them into conjunction at the right point. Arn gave a thrust, submerging the top of his tool. The elevated position I was in made his every move effective, and slowly he began to penetrate me. Soon, however, the head of his prick, which was now as hard as iron, came in contact with an obstruction which I supposed was my maidenhead. With a sudden plunge, still maintaining his grasp around my hips, he sent a cutting pain through my loins, making me gasp and groan, but I clenched my teeth and wriggled and heaved my bottom to meet him as I had seen Anne do. He was now in, full length, and I was maddened, intoxicated with a newly awakened lust. My passion was so great that even had I thought I should die from the pain, I would not have stopped him.

So instead of trying to escape, I spread my thighs still wider apart, and raising my legs in the air, I crossed them over his back, clasped my arms around his neck, and strained him to me with all my strength.

He drew back slightly and then drove forward slowly but firmly, and almost before I could realize it, his prick was gliding methodically in and out of the clinging folds of my cunt. The pain had now disappeared, being replaced with a wanton lust, particularly when his tool seemed to touch the very extremity of my cleft. He now began a steady, rocking motion which thrilled me with rapture and caused me to return his masterly thrusts with all my strength.

Ah, with what delight did I repay his delirious motions, working my loins and bottom to meet his as he drove in. I felt a blissful, overwhelming thrill, and everything swam before my eyes as I heaved up to meet his fierce thrusts and, with murmurs of delight, bathed his hot prick with my virgin emission. Just as I felt my senses bursting, the pulsating prick in my crevice gushed forth a copious discharge of hot fluid. The next thing I knew, Anne was sprinkling cologne in my face and chafing my hands. I was so overcome that I had to be assisted to sit on the edge of the bed.

Arn came over and sat down beside me and put his arm around my waist as I leaned weakly against him. Anne got water and towels and washed our sexual parts, bestowing caresses upon them as she did so.

We all got back on the bed, Arn lying between us, to enjoy a well-earned rest. As we lay with our heads on his shoulders and his arms clasping us, I felt I could stay there forever.

"Well, Daisy, how do you feel after your first fuck?" asked Arn. "I well recall when I had my first piece."

"And so do I," spoke Anne, "and I enjoyed myself as much as Daisy did, if not more. Suppose you tell us of your first adventure while we are resting." And with Arn's agreement, we settled ourselves comfortably with our hands placed on each other's lower parts as we prepared to listen to the story of Arn's first fuck.

CHAPTER NINE

IX

ARN'S STORY

I lived in the country when I was a boy, and one day my stepmother's cousin, a young widow, came to make us a summer visit. She was a fine-looking woman, about medium height, and splendidly proportioned. She had large, swelling breasts and a small waist with ample hips. The outline of her rounded thighs and tapered legs were more than suggested through the light summer dress which she wore.

These charms had an effect on my boyish mind to which I had hitherto been a stranger. Although mature, I had been kept pretty close at home, and being of a retiring nature, I had not mingled with the opposite sex. Of course, my imagination had often pictured the delights of copulation with girls, but of the reality I had no experience.

On the afternoon of her first day with us, my

father had to go into town and my mother was obliged to visit a sick neighbor, leaving me to entertain our guest. She expressed a desire to look over the farm and see the livestock. I was only too pleased to show her about. She had changed her clothes, and now wore a simple blouse and skirt. As the light breeze blew her skirt about, it was lifted to breathtaking heights. I even caught sight of unstockinged snow-white skin, showing me clearly that she wore nothing beneath that skirt. Going into the barn, she insisted on exploring every part of it for hen's nests and other barnyard surprises. She held her skirts high, and I had a number of beautiful views of her body. As she climbed about, I caught further glimpses of yellow garters and the glint of white skin above. You may be sure I was very careful not to let any of these new and singular sights escape my undivided attention; my fascinated eyes never missed a detail.

Walking through the orchard under the apple trees, we came to a brook which ran lazily through our farm. It eventually spread out into a broad pool which Father and I often used for bathing as it was surrounded by tall trees and quite private. On one side a fine stretch of sand sloped into the water to form an exquisite beach.

My companion went into raptures of delight over this picturesque pool. "I must certainly avail myself of the opportunity to bathe in this delectable pool while I am here. The water looks so cool and inviting, so tempting! If it weren't so much trouble, I'd take my clothes off and jump right in. I haven't had a wade since I was a child and used to go barefooted with the other girls of the neighborhood. I must try your pool. Speaking of girls, who is your sweetheart, Arn? Ah, how delicious this water feels! Come on in, Arn!"

She quickly removed her shoes and stockings, and had reached the water before I was fairly started. Hurrying to her side, I reached her just as she approached a spot where the pool took a drop of about a foot. She placed a hand on my shoulder just as her foot went into this hole, and as she felt herself falling she clutched at me with both hands. In her attempts to save herself, she lunged backwards, losing her balance and causing me to lose mine. In an instant we were both floundering in the water, soaked from head to foot.

Our one thought now being dry clothes, we hastened to the shore, gathered up our shoes and stockings, and returned to the house. She led the way, her figure distinctly outlined in the clinging folds of her wet garments, dripping water at every step. The soft material revealed every curve of her beautiful form, and it required very little imagination on my part to picture her unclothed figure in my mind.

We soon changed into dry clothing, and at the evening meal she caused considerable merriment by relating our sorry plight that afternoon as we returned from the pool. After kidding us about it my father said, "You may experience still more excitement while you are here. I have heard that a number of robberies have been committed near here lately, and several tramps have been seen in the neighborhood."

This information caused such consternation among

the ladies that Father hastened to add, "I don't think there is much danger, but I thought it best to tell you of it; chances are the thieves will have been rounded up by this time, as the officers have been searching for them diligently."

I retired as usual at my customary hour and was lying in bed clad in a nightshirt when I heard our guest come upstairs and enter her room across the hall. I heard her moving about for some time. Just as I was dozing off, her door opened softly and she approached mine. It opened and she entered. Although I knew who it was, I raised up and asked, "Who's there?"

"It's Hanna," she said, as she approached my bedside. "Oh, Arn, I simply can't get the idea of the burglars out of my mind. I'm so frightened! I want you to come and stay with me tonight. But you mustn't tell anyone, because I don't want them to laugh at me and ridicule us."

"All right, I'll stay with you if you want me to," I replied, hopping out of bed.

Taking my hand, she led me out of my room and into the darkness of hers. Once inside she closed and locked the door. The bed was near the window and the pale beams of the moon threw a soft light across it, making that spot almost as light as day. Quickly she got into bed and bade me follow. My feelings were almost beyond description when I found myself lying in bed beside this beautiful woman. I was at once elated and abashed and, while I longed to move over and clasp her in my arms, my juvenile fears held me in rigid check.

She, however, soon settled the matter. After keeping me a few minutes in suspense, she started. Placing one of my arms under her neck, she felt for and found the other which she drew over her lush breasts. With an arm under my neck, she began stroking my hair with her free hand. Bashfully, I groped over her breasts, becoming more bold as I heard no objections. Slipping my hand inside the opening of her nightgown, I laid it upon the bare flesh of one of the enchanting globes, the touch filling me with such emotion that I continued to fondle and squeeze it tenderly. Still meeting no objection, I opened the front wider and began to kiss and suck those delicious breasts. I continued this for some time until she said, "Arn, let's take off our things; the heat is most stifling." And disengaging her arm, she slipped from bed and drew off her nightie.

I was somewhat apprehensive as to what would be her impression of my cock when she saw its size and learned that I was more than a boy. Perhaps it would frighten her and she would call off my initiation, and this I wanted to avoid.

However, I stepped from the bed and removed my shirt, and as I turned toward her I was amazed at the voluptuous sight she presented, a ravishing form that would have seduced any man. She was entrancingly outlined in the moonlight. Dumb with admiration and ecstasy, I stood gazing at her.

Whatever reluctance I may have previously felt now vanished, and any latent impulse to flee was turned into an active desire to learn of those sensual delights created by such a seductive display.

"Arn! Arn! Come, get into bed! Don't stand there in the darkness. Come to bed—I won't bite you!"

I hastily complied with her request, still holding my nightshirt in front of my rigid cock (which was indeed one to be proud of). Slipping into bed, I also hastily slid out of reach. My position permitted me to look downward to the foot of the bed to keep out of reach of her groping hands. It also permitted me to look upon with ease and observe her broad belly and hips, soft as satin to the touch. Glancing at her cunny, I saw her soft mound covered with mossy hair.

Turning myself slightly, I moved my hand over her glowing form, patting and caressing it till I reached that hairy groove, then running my fingers through the soft fur until my tickling began to have a voluptuous effect on my fair bedfellow. My fingers went forward steadily till they reached the entrance of her grotto. Raising myself on my hand and elbow, I looked curiously at the spot that my hand was invading. I saw a cleft with luscious red lips which extended from the hairy mound down between her pretty thighs. This excited me, and I began to finger and fondle it.

All this time she had been smiling at my explorations and my rising excitement, as though she enjoyed the magnetic sensation she incited in me. Soon her quim began to respond to my touches and her feelings became aroused. She spread her legs apart, murmuring, "Get on top of me, Arn, and let's see what your little prick can accomplish."

I quickly moved up so that my chest rested on her belly and I could reach her lovely tits with my mouth. I began to kiss and suck them while I worked two fingers into her cleft. This had a terrific effect upon me, and I thought my prick would burst. My companion, judging from her wiggling, was also considerably affected.

"Come up higher, baby, and kiss me!" she murmured.

Eagerly raising myself to comply, the head of my cock reached her cunt and felt the warm juice which came from it. This was more than flesh could stand, and I began to push forward to force an entrance. She reached down—but not, as I had feared, to stop me. As she grasped my prick with one hand and opened the lips of her cunt with the other, she exclaimed in surprise, "My stars! Is that your prick?"

Its size astonished her, but her desires were too intense now to permit dawdling, and my own ardor was too deeply stirred to let anything to delay me. I pushed forward and entered, deep into those portals, and before either of us could think, the skin slipped back on my prick and it glided inside the warm passage. It was a tight fit, but I drove forward with determined strokes while she crossed her legs over my back.

Frantically, she heaved her bottom and tossed about. The fast movement quickly brought me to a crisis, while under me I felt her flesh clinging deliciously about my prick as I shoved in deep and hard. Soon the gates of bliss prepared to open, and my body trembled with the approach of ecstasy. I worked frantically, eagerly, with the single purpose of attaining that acme of delight and pleasure in this, my first ejaculation in a woman's grotto.

"Oh, darling, what bliss you are giving me! What joy, sweet child, what happiness is in store for me during this visit!"

I felt something thrilling taking place all along my shaft and gushing forth into her warm cunt. I worked rapidly, and with a final thrust shot forth the last drops of sperm. Everything went black before me, and I sank into blissful oblivion, fainting in her arms.

After we recovered our senses she asked me, as she fondled my prick, how old I was.

I told her.

"You little devil," she replied, as she took my cock in her mouth and sucked it hard again.

And that, dear girls, is the story of my first fuck.

We had listened to Arn's story with much pleasure and with ever-increasing lust. His prick, which I had been holding, had swollen until it now felt like an iron bar. I had been squeezing and tickling it all during the story while Anne had been gently caressing his balls.

"Oh, you rascal, you should have been ashamed to take advantage of a poor widow like that!"

"Well, she brought it on herself—indeed, it was she who took advantage of me!—but I don't think she felt the least bit penitent. However, the telling of the story has made me horny, dear girls, and I think that I am entitled to some recompense."

"I will be glad to soothe your inflamed cock in my burning crevice, as I have a peculiar feeling there myself."

"Oh, you had the last fuck!" protested Anne.

I had to be satisfied with this arrangement and watched Arn as he turned to Anne and began to caress her. They were both ready for action, and I was surprised to see Anne get on her hands and knees while Arn mounted her from behind. He laid well forward on her broad, white back, and with his arms in front, titillated her glorious breasts. I laid down with my head at their feet and watched their play as they twisted and wriggled. Arn let go of one of her titties and, reaching over, plunged his fingers in and out of my burning slit.

Their blissful moment approached, and he shot his load into her rapacious cunt, after which they maintained their novel position for a few moments while he gave several twists with his throbbing prick, and then collapsed.

CHAPTER TEN

X

ANNE'S STORY

Like Arn, I lived in the country when I was a girl. One summer day I was alone while my parents went to town for supplies.

After dinner, I was reading a novel when I was called on by Johnny, one of the farmer boys, a lad considerably younger than I who lived down the road on the adjoining farm. He was a good-looking, curly haired chap, and since he was hot and tired from his journey, I invited him to sit on the porch and rest. I sat down beside him and began to tease him. At first he resented my joking, but finally he allowed me to hug and caress him, and soon I had him sitting on my lap. My kisses caused his face to flush, but he placed his arm around my neck and returned them. I was getting along wonderfully.

I had never seen a boy's thing, and as my feelings

rose I grew wanton, and determined to see one now or die in the attempt. Getting up, I said, "Let's go inside the house, Johnny. I have something to show you."

He followed me into the parlor, where I sat upon the sofa and told him to stand in front of me. He obeyed, and I asked him if he knew I had a bird's nest between my legs. This naturally aroused his curiosity—as I intended it should!—and he asked if he could see it.

"I will, if you let me see the thing you pee with."

He agreed and let me unbutton his pants. I lowered them, pulled up his shirt, and took hold of his inexperienced little prick. Flaccid as it was, it nevertheless greatly interested me, especially since it grew harder under my touch. That made me hotter still. Lying back on the sofa, I pulled up my skirts and exposed my cunny to his curious gaze. I wore no panties. He seemed entranced, standing there looking at the first cunt his eyes had ever beheld, then gazing at his own organ, as though wondering why they were so different.

"Put your hand on it, Johnny, and see how funny it feels."

He did so at once. I told him to tickle it, and in this he also obeyed, though in a nervous manner. This did not cool my desires, and opening my legs I lay back and told him to get on me and I would show him something else interesting. He did as I suggested, and I soon had his prick lying right against the crack intended to receive it. I had just reached down and grasped it, preparatory to inserting it within the golden gates, when I heard a step in the room and, looking up, found to my horror that a man was looking down at us.

"Merciful Gabriel!" I exclaimed, pushing Johnny roughly aside and sitting up, jerking down my clothes at the same time. Imagine my horror to discover that the intruder was our preacher, who visited the neighborhood once a month. What was I to do?

He was a stern, middle-aged man, tall and rawboned, with a large frame. He wore his beard trimmed and was well-dressed for our part of the country. I sat speechless with shame and mortification, my face in my hands, awaiting his denunciation. I expected no mercy from this paragon of righteousness. No doubt he would also make a report to my parents, and I would be severely punished.

"Well, I am astonished beyond words to see you indulging in a carnal orgy—the very cesspool of sin! Alas, I am grieved at what I saw! I have always thought of you as one of our womanly angels," with which he made a magnificent gesture. "Now I see you are like Delilah, seducing this juvenile Samson. Alas, the sins of the flesh! I came upon you softly, expecting to find you engaged in some innocent pastime and intending to give you a pleasant surprise. I had hoped to enjoy the pleasure of a discourse on heavenly piety and its reward in the mansion of the skies. But what disillusionment! I find you engaged in the ancient gluttonies of sinful Rome. Ah, heavy is my heart within me this day!"

Then turning to the bewildered youth who stood trembling and in fear he said sternly, "Young man, put on your garment and be gone. But wait...don't say anything about this, or the wrath of Jehovah will

gratified, and it will be such a shock to your nerves that you will never again be tempted to seduce a boy. I shall go through the actions to show you the enormity of your offense."

I looked at him in surprise as his purpose slowly dawned upon me. He, noting my anxiety, added that it was given to ministers of the gospel to have the privilege of using all just means of disciplining their charges.

"Still, if I tell your father, he will punish you most severely, and I would also have to make mention of this most terrible affair from the pulpit tomorrow. Perhaps, after all, it would be better if I followed the line of least resistance."

"Oh, goodness! No! No! Anything else...!"

I had a mental picture of my father's face before me, and his intense disgust at the idea of my having fallen into carnal sin. I much preferred whatever form of shaming punishment the preacher might inflict. I rather fancied from his words and a certain gleam in his eyes that it might be more agreeable than not.

"Please don't tell my father," I implored. I threw my arms about his neck, taking care as I did so to still seem meek and contrite. "I will do anything...only don't tell!"

"Very well, if that is your choice. We'll begin at the beginning," he answered, as he hugged me to him. His face flushed and his eyes shone with what, my feminine instinct assured me, was burning desire.

He began to kiss and squeeze me. He unbuttoned my dress, thrust his hand inside the bodice, and fondled my titties, which made a good handful. Under his caresses I lost my awe of him and hugged him passionately, returning his hot kisses with gusto. Opening my dress wide, his let his lips and tongue wander all over my breasts, thrilling me with excitement. Suddenly he released me and told me to stand up in front of him and unbutton his trousers. Through the material I could already see the outline of something that was trying to get out. In another moment I had pulled up his shirt and gotten my first view of a grown man's cock. As it burst forth from its confinement and pointed right up at me, I saw the huge bag hanging below it. What a difference between this one and Johnny's! I could not resist the temptation to take it in my hand. I squeezed and pressed it and drew back the skin which covered its ruby head, bending forward to note every detail of the object. The sight filled me with a mad desire to have it in me, and I felt that I could endure with pleasure any pain accompanying its insertion.

The preacher arose and went to a chair to remove his shoes. "In order to make the lesson complete, we will take everything off and I will show you what you richly deserve."

I was barefooted and it didn't take me long to remove the few clothes I was wearing, and was soon as naked as Eve in the Garden of Eden. As I finished undressing, he slipped his shirt off, and now I really feasted my eyes on his enormous tool. He came over quickly and, picked me up, hugging me to his bosom while he showered hot kisses on my face, neck, and breasts. Laying me on my back on the sofa, he stood for a moment regarding my glowing body as I lay trembling between fear and desire. He stood so only briefly, then laid himself gently upon me. He got his knees between my legs, forcing them apart, as he slipped one hand under my body and the other around my neck. As his immense cock pulsed warmly against my belly, I reached down and commenced to caress it.

He drew back, but driven by a desire for relief, I rubbed the head of his prick against my cunt. He began to push and, releasing my hold on his cock, I threw both arms around his neck. I felt the head of his cock penetrate the lips of my crack. It entered slowly, inch by inch. The sensation was so overwhelming that I lost control of myself, and forgetting the pain his member was causing me, I drew my feet up and heaved and thrusted to meet his drives. His fierce plunges soon sent the quivering prick into my very vitals; and my cunt was gorged with pleasure. Nine inches of prick was soaking in my cunt, and I tasted the voluptuous rod quivering and shooting warm sperm into my very womb.

I can scarcely describe the emotions I felt at that moment. Our bodies were so closely entwined, and his prick so quivered and throbbed as it shot out jet after jet of the true Balm of Gilead, that I trembled with joy from head to toe while my breasts heaved, and we both moaned and gasped with ecstasy. It seemed to me as if the whole of his prick were dissolving within me. He tossed and rolled about, his eyes becoming glassy. It was unbearable, human nature could stand no more, and I fainted away with the consciousness of the hot answering gush within my own body.

When I revived, my cunt was no longer itching; it

had at last been soothed with the divine essence. Of course, more of this followed, but that is another story. This ends the tale of my first and most delightful fuck, administered to me by our preacher as a form of chastisement.

Anne's story had excited me to a high pitch, and I raised myself and threw the upper part of my body across Arn's chest.

"Fuck me, Arn darling, fuck me!" I implored.

Arn pulled me into position. Anne took his cock and presented its head to my moist opening. I was dying for this one and settled down softly as it plunged into the fiery passage. I galloped up and down fiercely for a couple of minutes until Nature quickly reduced our fires with a soothing emission. I lay for some time without moving, his cock buried in the wet depths of my crevice.

Anne lay quietly, looking on at our passion, her hand gently fingering her cunt. She glanced at the clock, saw that it would soon be daylight, and said that it behooved Arn to make his getaway. When she admonished us to hasten and separate, he jumped up and hurriedly dressed. After bestowing an affectionate kiss upon each of us, he departed.

I then slipped back into my own room and prepared to snatch a few winks of sleep before I appeared for breakfast.

And so, dear diary, you hold in your pages the secret shared only by myself and two others. It has been the most thrilling experience of my life, but I sincerely hope to have many more such good times to describe on your pages in the near future.

CHAPTER ELEVEN

XI

There was no more of interest in the diary. Since this entry was dated only a short time previously, the owner was no doubt still looking forward to a repetition of her experiences. Under these circumstances, I determined to return the book in person the following day. Accordingly, I dressed to my best advantage and I started out, not without some trepidation, to find the residence of the diarist, Daisy Collinsworth.

The address proved to be that of a very pretentious place, and I felt a little nervousness—only natural under the circumstances—as I hastened up the steps, rang the bell, and waited impatiently. The door was opened by a buxom and exceptionally pleasant-looking maid, who politely asked me my business. Upon my inquiring for Miss Daisy, she smiled and bade me enter.

I had barely seated myself in the elegantly furnished reception room when a light step announced the appearance of Miss Daisy. She was indeed attractive, and stylishly dressed as if ready to go for a walk. I asked if she were Miss Daisy and she replied in the affirmative, looking at me curiously, and inquiring what she could do for me. I informed her that I had, on the day previous, picked up a book of hers; and had called to return it.

Her consternation was apparent and I produced the book at once. I allowed her to see it, but did not yet relinquish it.

"Oh, yes, it is mine!" she exclaimed, blushing. "I hadn't missed it. It must have slipped from my pocketbook. Where did you find it?"

I told her, and then added, "It was indeed most interesting. I read some of your entries with particular relish."

She blushed furiously and said, "Oh, you did not pry into it any more than was necessary, did you?"

"No, but some of the entries held my attention for more than a moment, and from the general tenor I felt that the owner would rather have the book in her possession."

"Oh, I knew you read it through!"

"Well, my dear young lady, wasn't I obliged to open it to get your address?"

"Yes, to be sure."

"Well, then, seeing a sentence that arrested my attention, I naturally read further. Anyone under similar circumstances would have read it, and particularly the entry of August 25th. That was indeed interesting."

"You must think me a most degraded person."

"Not at all!"

"Oh!" She was all confusion and shame. "What must you think of me? Please do not mention this incident to anyone; if my parents were to be acquainted with what I have written about in my diary—or even that I was aware of the affairs of married folk—I would be disgraced forever."

I merely smiled and maintained a deep silence.

She had already been blushing, but now she turned rosier still. "What would you ask of me—in pledge of your silence?" she murmured shyly, peeping up at me through her lashes.

I ignored this interesting sally and said, "Miss Daisy, I am not of the opinion that you are an awful person, nor that you are the least bit degraded. In fact, you are a ravishingly beautiful creature, and what you did was only natural. Ahhh..." I sighed, "if only I had been in Arn's place that night!" Feeling that I now had the situation well in hand, I reclined in a comfortable chair.

Daisy caught my suggestion with demure alacrity and came and sat by my side. Then she placed a hand on my shoulder and smiled at me meaningfully. "If you will promise not to tell, I will treat you well. Promise me that you will not reveal any of the information which you have gleaned from the pages of my diary—please!"

She looked at me so bewitchingly that even had I been of a sneaky nature, my heart would have melted. "Yes, my dear, you may rest assured that I shall never reveal your secrets. I shall treasure my information as a sacred trust between us forever."

She flashed a grateful smile at me and drew closer. "Give me a kiss," I said, "and we will talk this over more deeply."

Leaning over, I placed an arm about her pretty waist and drew her unresisting body to me. I pulled her head down on my shoulder and shortly she was returning my rapturously bestowed kisses. She sighed and moaned with pleasure and crept closer to me, snuggling her voluptuous body up to mine with all the appeal at her command. Reaching down, I lifted her dress to her knees and began to fondle her legs, starting at the ankles and working my way up to her thighs. Her legs were indeed of most perfect contour and shape. I let my hand linger as I caressed them.

Her flesh glowed under my touch, and she quivered with unconcealed emotion. My hand stole beneath her bloomers and upward between her thighs, resting a moment on her mount and the moist, silky valley below. By now my blood was on fire and my fevered tool was begging to be released. I played and toyed with the soft curls, then parted the humid lips and permitted my fingers to intrude and explore her most secret recesses. I pressed and fingered the rigid clitoris with a passion-provoking touch that soon brought her excitement to such a pitch that she began unbuttoning my trousers. She opened them most delicately and reached inside with her dainty white hand.

This caused my prick to swell and throb madly. She molded and caressed it in a most intoxicating manner. It grew hard, almost exploding in an outburst of rapture at the thrilling sensations her hand produced. It demanded instant relief. Rising, I caught her in my arms and carried her to a large couch. She expressed a fear that someone might come in, but I urged that something be done quickly to relieve our passions.

She nodded her agreement, saying then, "Oh, I am in as great a rush as you are—but I have an idea."

As she rolled off the couch, there was a momentary flash of white as the superfluous bloomers were whisked off and stuffed behind a sofa cushion. After bending over, she threw her clothing up over her back and spread her legs apart, presenting a sight at once so lovely and intoxicating as to make my head swim.

"Come and do it this way!" she whispered. "We will not muss our clothes and will be ready on an instant's notice to adjust ourselves if anyone approaches."

Bent forward as she was, her entire upper torso had disappeared from my view. That portion left to my gaze was nevertheless exquisite. Her legs were long and finely formed; her calves and thighs and buttocks, pulled and shaped by her bending, were hard and smooth above her high-heeled feet. Her translucent black silk stocking-tops reached to midthigh, and her firm, white flesh spilled out over their tight fit and rose smoothly up to her haunches.

From the tip of her spine at the top of this lovely landscape, a fine dark rivulet of flesh traced a path between the well-proportioned hills of her buttocks. The line broadened into a pond of delight at her quivering bumhole, an enticing entryway to a cavern I chose to reserve for later exploration. Below this spread-wide anal coffer the line flowed together again briefly, finally blending into the channels and levees of her sopping quim.

This most tempting delicacy hung heavy beneath her firm belly, expectantly awaiting my touch, its lips parted just a measure to expose the juicy pink rewards inside.

I was instantly in position behind her and could not resist the temptation, eager as I was, of planting a luscious sucking kiss on the pretty cunt before proceeding to the further business at hand.

Thrusting my prick between her rounded thighs, I began to prod the entrance to her grotto and quickly found myself inside in a moist and delightful retreat. My aim was good, for the head slid instantly into place. With a firm stroke, I buried it to the balls.

As I pushed and thrust, I felt myself nearing climax. Grabbing her thighs, I pulled her firmly against me as, with a heavy lunge, I poured the essence of love in hot and copious gushes into her cunt.

I was about to withdraw when I was startled to see someone behind me. It was the very maid who had opened the door for me but a short time before. I was much relieved, for I had thought it was one of the family.

Miss Daisy raised herself to look and said quietly, "Oh, Anne, how you frightened me. I thought you were in the kitchen!"

Realizing at once that the intruder was Anne of the diary, I knew I was on safe ground. I drew Anne to me, raised her skirts, and felt her cunt. She did not object. Recalling Anne's part in the episode in Daisy's diary had already brought my cock to attention, and I said, "Anne, how about you? Are you afraid of mussing your clothes, or can you be prevailed upon to enjoy a good fuck?"

"Go ahead, big boy." She laughed at me merrily. "I haven't a dime's worth of underclothes on anyway!"

CHAPTER TWELVE

XII

Dear Reader: Did you enjoy that little tale Betty's father told us over a number of nights? We did, I assure you, and took turns acting out the parts and recreating the scenes and encounters as he related them to us. Here is another tale that became one of my favorites. As Betty's father would tell it, I would act out the part of the female. Betty would sometimes get the old reliable dildo and perform the manly positions. Sometimes she would just caress her father as he recounted the tale. How you enjoy the story, I leave to you.

From my secret observatory—a tiny perforation in the wall, just below the molding, which enabled me to clandestinely observe the movements of my neighbors in the adjoining suite—I had, for five consecutive afternoons, witnessed a most impressive scene.

The occupants of the suite in reference were a married couple. The woman, whose singular beauty had originally inspired me with the idea of violating the privacy of her boudoir via my peephole, could not have been over twenty-five at the most, and was possessed of a face and form which even the most fastidious critic would have pronounced faultless. Dark, exotically beautiful, she was a Latin Venus in miniature. Her long lashes shadowed eyes of deepest violet; her lips, scarlet beyond the need for rouging, seemed formed for lingering kisses.

In direct antithesis to this brunette flower was a husband many years her senior, a silent, stern-visaged man in whose veins the fires of youth had long since ceased to burn. They were an incongruous and oddly mated pair, an alliance of convenience, possibly; and one which I suspected weighed heavily upon the beautiful shoulders of the young wife. During the entire period I had observed them in their hours of privacy, I never saw a single demonstration of an amorous nature.

Their lives were nevertheless peaceful and regular. The husband arose early each morning and departed by nine o'clock, returning late in the evening.

The wife arose later, lingering an hour or more with her toilette, then also left the suite, returning always in the middle of the afternoon, at which time she changed from her street clothes, bathed, and spent the rest of the afternoon in the comfort of a beautiful silk negligee. She had no callers and no visitors, nor did she vary the routine I have described except on rare occasions.

Day by day I enjoyed the indescribable thrill of watching the beautiful and exotic creature as she dressed or undressed, and more than once was fortunate enough to glimpse a vision of nude loveliness which caused me to hold my breath in sheer admiration, while my heart pounded in response to the emotions her nudity evoked.

Naturally, when I perforated the wall, I had anticipated expansive spectacles of voluptuous conjugal pleasure. Strangely, then, that nothing of the kind had transpired within my range of vision, and I had been rewarded for my pains only with visions of nudity or partial nudity so chaste that they might well have been transferred to canvas without arousing sentiments other than those of purest admiration. This was all, until...

She came in hurriedly one afternoon around four. There was a lightness to her step and a look upon her face which suggested that she was under the spell of some pleasant emotion. Removing her chic little hat, but without changing from her street clothes as was customary, she withdrew from her purse what appeared to be a folded letter. Seating herself in a small rocking chair near the curtained windows, she spread the pages out on her lap and began to read.

It was evident that the perusal of this letter, if such it was, afforded her the greatest satisfaction, for as her violet eyes eagerly devoured the written words, her face became radiant, and a tender smile hovered about her lips. As she neared what seemed to be the concluding paragraphs of the voluminous epistle, her face became violently flushed. She threw her head back and closed her eyes, as though prey to some overwhelming motion. For a moment she remained motionless, with the still-unread last pages clutched in trembling fingers upon her lap. For an interval of thirty seconds, perhaps, the picture remained thus. Then her right hand moved down to the hem of the black skirt which clung about her knees. With a delicate gesture she drew the loose folds upward, above the tops of her hose, until half of her thighs were exposed. Shifting her body slightly to attain a more recumbent position, she separated her legs and extended them almost straight outward. The next moment her right hand disappeared between the parted thighs, lost within the folds of the concealing garments.

When the vibration of her wrist and forearm subsided fifteen or twenty seconds later, she shook her skirts back into place and resumed reading the letter. Upon concluding it, she toyed with it tenderly, finally raising it to her lips to press passionate kisses upon the inanimate pages.

Now, following her interrupted custom, she disrobed, spent an hour in the bathroom out of my sight, and reappeared dressed in a dainty negligee, hose of golden brown silk, and tiny mules. She went immediately to her writing desk, and with the letter before her which had so stirred her emotions, began the composition of a reply. She wrote in a distracted fashion, pausing for long periods to gaze into space, but in the course of an hour she'd managed to cover several pages. Gathering these in her hands, she leaned back and began to read. As she did so, the telltale flush again stole over her face. Suddenly dropping the letter, she rose to her feet, stripped off the gossamer gown, and threw herself upon the sofa.

She masturbated again, this time in the wildest and most furious manner.

When her solitary pleasure was concluded and the heaving of her breasts had subsided, she rose. Taking the first letter she had read, and the pages she had written, she folded them and placed them between the leaves of a book. She knelt on the floor by the sofa and inserted the book in some hidden recess among the springs or in its framework.

For five consecutive days I watched her progress in composing this mysterious letter, as she alternately masturbated and wrote. I became determined to see both those letters, regardless of risk or consequences. On the fifth afternoon, I gathered from certain indications that the composition was finished, so it was only a question of whether or not it would be mailed before I could steal it.

I watched her movements anxiously the following day as she prepared to leave the suite. To my joy, she did not remove the manuscript from its hiding place when she took her customary departure.

I waited a discreet interval, then entered the room with the aid of a passkey and went to the sofa. After a bit of fumbling, I found the hidden volume where the letters were concealed, extracted them, replaced the book, and returned quickly to my room. In less than two hours I had made copies of the letters and restored the originals to their hiding place.

My Darling:

A frantic hunger for you is upon me; my whole body is one raging, aching desire for your embraces.

Answer me, my darling—respond somehow, with your body reaching out for mine. Let me know, by some answering blaze of passion in your eyes, that the power of your sex is aroused. Show me by the tense pressure of your lips against mine, by your quickened pulse, the clutching of your hands, the movement of your knees to embrace me, that satisfaction awaits me. I want you burning with the knowledge that you are a woman, unable to rest until you have taken me entirely to yourself and, by the sweet uses of your body, given and received relief.

Beloved, reach out your hand, with impatient fingers undo a few buttons, and something will spring forth, tense, into your welcoming grasp. Do you know what it is? It is manhood, the male element, seeking to fertilize the female and so bear fruit. When the male passion moves and stirs, seeking the woman, this grows turgid, it swells, becomes large, stiffens and grows hard. It rises, throbbing with impatient pulses. It seems to know that its function is to enter, to penetrate; it seeks something that is wonderfully its opposite.

Substantial, it has dimensions, it fills a certain space. It must push and enter, the female open and receiving. Eternal opposites, male and female, find in their union a completeness!

How does it feel in your hand, sweetheart? As your fingers close around it, holding it, feeling its heat, its strength, does any part of your dear body thrill and throb to its call? You are a woman, the female spirit is in you; does something in your flesh quiver with answering desire? How does it feel, dear, when you find me thus, and you long to clasp me to you? What is your sensation? Is there a part of you that is empty, that longs to be filled? Has it nerves, dear, and sensitive, delicate surfaces that suffuse, itch; that want to be tickled, touched, and rubbed?

Between your lovely legs, my sweet, my desire, there is a part of your body covered with dark, curly hair, growing upward to the lower part of your soft stomach, spreading out in soft curls, an enticement! I desire you naked, my beloved. I wish to behold my dearest woman and wonder at the curving, lovely lines of her body, so graceful and rich. That cluster of curly hair fascinates and entices me. My fingers reach out to touch it. I am close to you, darling. I, too, have hair on me, around this thing your hand holds. Run your fingers through my hair there, as I run mine through yours. We look and see our fingers playing with the curls, our bodies close together so that the dark hair mingles.

Part your legs a little, sweetheart, as I part mine, so that my fingers may feel you there as you feel me, touching, stroking, tickling, caressing! Oh, it feels so good!

Sit by me, dear, spread your legs before me, all widely open to my hand. As I fondle you between the legs, so you fondle me, and as we watch our hands at play, our desire for each other grows. Between wonder-giving kisses we let our eyes drink in the fascination of our bodies thus together, your soft, white legs and my firm, hairy ones, your hands and mine, and what the hands touch and caress. I love it, dear, to see your nakedness as well as feel it, to see you all exposed to my inquiring fingers; to see your lovely breasts, full and firm, to see the whiteness of you; to see your fingers play upon me, and what my own fingers touch; but most of all, my wonder, to see the gladness in your face, your laughter, your enjoyment of this wanton play. You love to be naked with me and to play with me this way, do you not, my darling?

Let me lie upon you, dearest, with my head between your legs. Rest your head and shoulders between my knees. This thing that you love swings there, close before your mouth. Take it in your hands and bring it to your lips. I love the touch of your lips upon it! Kiss it, darling, run your wet tongue over it and lick it. Take it in your mouth and suck it, suck it! Oh, the sensation is wonderful! And as you suck, my tongue will softly lick you, exploring the spot that is most responsive. Will you like that, darling?

I crave you so, crave all that you can and will do to satisfy my burning desire for you. And I long to do all that I can to meet your desires, to fill your body with as much delight as you give me, to pour upon you all the caresses, kisses, touches, movements, that can arouse your sex to quivering, palpitating joy. I want your hands, your mouth, your breasts, your legs, and what is between your legs, to take me, hold me, draw me, suck me, engulf me, arouse me with soft, delicate frictions. I want you to arouse and kindle and excite me with more and more ardent movements of your body, closer, hotter embraces of your arms and legs, wetter and more delirious kisses, until I can stand no more, until with a final crushing thrust I will take you, with a thrill beyond all thrills. For one still moment my forces will seem gathered for a charge, every muscle straining, arms and legs tense.

Then, with spasmodic spurts, each one a delirium of bliss, my hot floods will leap in gushing jets against your womb!

Dear, my fingers in their play have touched the neck of your womb, but that other part of me, not yet. Some day, some night, we shall find a posture which will bring your womb's mouth so that I may thrust hard against it. Then, indeed, there will be a contact, a touch, a kiss of sex to sex within your body! That will bring a completeness, a perfection of sensation, a heaven of bliss, a surpassing wonder of delight, a perfect realization of the sensuous joys of love between man and woman!

How I love your naked body and all its delights! Can there be anything about the body of a man, I wonder, that can so thrill a woman as your naked beauty thrills me? Could you put your hand on me now and feel how my desire and the writing of this has made me hard? Part your legs, dear, and let me push it into you, in, in, then I'll draw it out, almost entirely out, tickling you outside, then in again. Look, dear, watch it going in and coming out again. Hold your legs high, darling, so that you come up to meet me, put your legs over my shoulders, and then watch how I push down into you! Oh, the fascination of having you there, beneath me, your beautiful, soft legs about me. There is such laughter and happiness in our loveplay! My darling, my adored, my sweetheart, my beautiful, my love mate, my lovely, naked, happy woman!

You are wonderful in the response you make to me. I love the utter abandon with which you surrender the whole of your dear body to our play, the happy wantonness with which you laugh as you take off your clothing, unashamed, before my eyes, and step naked and ripe for love into my eager arms. I love the gladness of you, your quips and pranks, your playful ways in our first cuddling embraces, and then, as our passion grows upon us, your fierce enjoyment of every way in which woman and man can take and give the sensuous joys of love. Altogether mine, my wonder and delight! And I am altogether yours.

See, it is still hard and big as I go on writing! Hard for your body, my darling, my only one! Do you remember the afternoon that I sat in the little rocking chair and you came and sat on me? No, you did not sit on me, you bestrode me and impaled yourself on me. How you laughed with delight! When shall I see you again and find that sweet and loving welcome, that ardent embrace, that ready, eager kiss, that dear delight of holding you in my arms, that quickly kindled fire of desire, that sweet, glad surrender to passion? How long before I may whisper to you again that I love you, love you, oh, my heart's darling, that I love you and adore you? That time must come, beloved, when I shall take you all to myself, if only for a day, and reach out more and more in unceasing love, unending wonder. Evade your husband somehow, sweetheart, and come to your own true lover for hours of bliss!

Dearest, if I cry out for the delights of love in your sweet embraces, it is not wholly selfish; it is partly because I know your ardor and so I wish to serve you with my body as you serve me, to give as I receive. Our joy must be mutual, or it is no real joy at all. We have had so much, so much! But not enough, darling, not nearly enough, is that not so? Do you not wish more and more, my love, of that dear happiness that we find only when we two are together and may give free expression to our mutual desires?

Is not desire for my love and kisses so great that it may not remain desire, but becomes fulfillment all by itself? Do not my words arouse you to a pitch of frenzy, so that you quiver and thrill and tingle all over? Tell me this, do you not draw up your clothes and part your legs and put your hand in there and find yourself hot and wet?

When you read that I have something for you, standing up big and hard, do you not wish that you could take it in your hand and feel it all over, and rub it, and put it to your lips, and take it in your mouth and then put it between your legs, to have it go in? With your legs apart, do you not itch and tingle as you think of that big, stiff thing moving inside you, taking pleasure in you? Do you not want to be all naked, tossing hot and breathless in my arms, while the big, hard tickler and teaser touches and pushes and makes you more and more frantic? Do you not wish you could eat me up with love, jump on me, and suck me up into yourself?

Darling, it is straight and big and throbbing for you this minute. Its head is dark red with the blood that pulses into it at the thought of you. It wants your fingers touching it, clasping it, rubbing it up and down, pulling the skin up over the end of it and then pulling it back down. It wants you tickling all around it, through the hair that grows over its base, your fingers, feeling, touching tickling everywhere!

Dearest, it wants to push against your soft little

curly haired kit, to push and knock and tap and tickle and tease there until the doors open and it slips into your secret garden. And, darling, you would like to feel it running about in there, wouldn't you? Would it give you thrills, waves of tingles and throbs, floods of joy such as you know only when your own lover is in your arms, between your legs, thrusting and pushing into you, holding you close and dear?

That is what it is for, beloved, to give my own sweetheart all the joys of passionate love that I can. Do you want it? Do you need it filling you until you overflow in rushing floods of overwhelming pleasure?

Oh, if it could only stand up for you all one night, and never get tired, but go on hour after hour, exhausting you, satiating you, yet ready and eager to give you more as soon as you had rested awhile and wanted it again! Think of us lying together, naked in the pale moonlight, your golden body against my darker skin! Think of the twining of legs and arms, of the close, warm embraces, of the kisses that would crush your breasts and crowd upon your mouth, of the sweet, lewd, magic words of love and desire, of the movements and pressures of our hips—your lovely legs apart, I kneeling between them. We would see together those tangled curls of hair on your body, and the black patch on mine, with my own joymaker standing out big and firm amidst it. And I would come down, closer and closer, and you would raise your head and see how it came nearer and nearer, then touched, then pushed an instant, and then went slowly into you until it was swallowed up! Then you would watch it go in and out, like a ramrod loading you with love, until you could not stand it any longer. And then you would lie back on the pillow, seize me with your lovely arms and pull me down on you, and cram my thirsty mouth with eager kisses, and throw your beautiful legs around me and hold me close, and heave and twist your hips to get more of the delicious rubbing, and my arms would go under you, lifting your hips and forcing you against me while I pushed and heaved and thrust and rubbed, until, until, until…

Then, after a little rest, with sweet kisses, telling each other how good it was, a soft voice would say, "John, darling man, I want it again!" And your hand would find it ready, big and hard as ever, and your body would cover me.

A whole, never-ending night of it is what your lover would like to give to his sweetheart, to have for himself. I wonder if your teasing, tickling joymaker could do it, could stand it? Would my darling like to try it if she could?

Does this call for an answer, dear?

My Dearest Beloved:

Your wonderful letter has thrilled me from top to toe; I am afire, my blood is racing, my mind is a confusion of sensuous pictures. How can you write so, put all these things in words that make them seem as if they are actually happening? But they are not happening; I only wish they were. I am your sweetheart; we have been everything to each other. I have given myself to you, I am yours; and you have been dear and good to me, and tender and gentle, and I feel that you are mine. I am going to write and tell you so, tell you how deeply I feel that we belong to each other, even if we are married to other people. And I am going to show you, shamelessly, just what kind of a woman I am, so that you will know (if you do not know it already) that underneath my civilized exterior I am just a plain woman, with appetites and desires which only the use of my sex can satisfy.

Dearest, until you came I did not know that desire could be satisfied. My husband (forgive me for bringing him in, dear) takes me whenever he wants me; he has always come to me when he felt that way, and taken me, and satisfied himself, but he never satisfied me. You have shown me a new heaven and a new earth, a new life, a new meaning of love, a whole new universe of experience, all unimagined by me. You see, I knew nothing until you taught me. I married young. I thought that what I experienced with my husband was normal. I liked him; I even thought I loved him. I was glad to be nice to him and to have him take me in bed; that was what wives were for. But, ignorant as I was, I could never understand the hints and suggestions of other women that there was any great pleasure in having a husband to be in bed with; I thought that they, these other women, got a good deal of enjoyment out of a very uninteresting thing. You see, I thought that their experience was the same as mine.

What an ignorant thing I was! The first time I saw you I had a feeling that you were different; the first time I touched your hand I had a thrill that no other man had ever given me. The first time I looked into your eyes I was frightened at the strange desire to kiss you! My darling lover that you are, how gently you led me from one thing to another until I knew I wanted nothing so much in the world as to be in your arms!

Yes, I have been in your arms, in such rapture as I have never dreamed of. Yes, we have been flesh to flesh, and I have learned something of what that may mean. Yes, I can feel you now, I can feel your hands on me, on my arms, breasts, legs...oh, my dearest, what can I not feel on reading your wonderful letter! You call up such pictures....

I shall never, never forget you as you sat in that chair, inviting me to come to you. You sat there naked, and I could see all of you, all that I craved. I can see you now! I see your strong arms outstretched for me. I see the eager, devouring look in your ardent eyes. I see your broad chest with the dark hair. I see the curly black hair that runs down your abdomen and the big, black patch below. But above all, I see the wonderful thing that transforms me, that makes me an elemental woman, aching with sex. So huge and strong it stands and calls to me, calls more commandingly than your waiting arms, than your devouring eyes. I must come to you quickly and feel that tremendous thing in my body!

My lover! Even in writing to you I feel that I must be yours. I had to stop and take off my clothes. What do you think of that? I am not quite naked, I have on my stockings and slippers. As I go on writing I feel that you can see me, my breasts that you love so, my legs and all, and there is no part of my body that your hands cannot easily touch and caress. But I feel that I am naked, too, as I was that afternoon when I first stood before you, naked from head to foot.

Look at me, my man, as your woman comes to you! Look at me as I stand here. Do you desire me? Am I fair to your eyes? Oh, I want to be beautiful, desirable to you. Take my breasts in your hands as I lean over you, letting them fall into your grasp. Take my lips with your kiss, caress my body, run your hands over my hips, clasp my waist, my bottom, my thighs, as I part my legs and come astride you! I want your fingers to play around my legs and between them, tickling my hair. I want you to fondle me there and find how ready I am for you, hot and wet and open.

Oh, my darling, as I sit here, writing all this to you, my legs are parted. Your hand is not between them, but one of mine is, and my fingers feel those hot, wet lips that your fingers should be feeling. I can hardly write; see how shaky the letters are.

I am astride you, my beloved. Let me hover here a moment, to gather this heavenly wonder from the touch of your fingers. My body quivers with it! Oh, how I love you and want you! Gather my kisses, love, my wet, clinging kisses! Kiss my breasts with your hot mouth, kiss them, draw out and suck gently on my sensitive nipples! But do not stop that marvelous touching, sliding, tickling, pressing of your fingers. Touch that little place that you say gets hard, press it just a little (my own finger is doing it for you)! Oh! I cannot wait, darling, I must sit on you and suck that great, hard thing into myself, in—in—in!

Look, beloved, look and see how close we are! See your hair and mine. Our fingers meet and play together there. Oh, how I love that soft, low laugh of yours at our delicious play! Kiss me, kiss me, kiss me!

Your hands are all over me. You love your naked, wanton sweetheart in this wild, sweet play. Your lips, my lips, cling and move; your tongue, my tongue, suck and quiver, yours in my mouth, mine in yours. Our bodies are crushed together. Oh, I love it, love it, oh, how I love it all!

Forgive me if you can hardly read this; my left hand is so busy, touching, pressing between my naked legs, I cannot spare it to hold the paper straight. I am so aroused, wild, mad with desire!

See, I am astride you, and move with my hips, darling. Is it good, my sweet man, my beloved whom I love with my whole body, does it feel good to you? You are the core of me, filling me; I move deliciously upon you, deliciously, exquisitely! Oh, it feels so good, so good, oh, I love it! I am wild for you!

Rock with me, my darling, as you did that afternoon. Oh, the rubbing as we sway, back and forth, as that astonishing thing slides a little in and out of me! My big man likes that, too, to have this loving, naked woman impaled on him, rocking back and forth. Your kisses tell me so, and your hands that wander over my body. I love to give you my body; all of it is yours, beloved, yours to love, yours to enjoy, to use for your pleasure. Your joy in me is becoming my own greatest delight and happiness. I am your woman—use my body as it pleases you!

Oh, I love you! I love this sitting on you, astride you, my legs apart, impaled on you! I like it better even than lying under you in bed, or lying on you. But I love everything you do, every attitude, every posture in which we can join, naked together, you and I, doing all these wild, mad things.

Oh, dear, you are hundreds of miles away, and I sit here just dripping for you! That's not very nice, but it's true. I'm dripping, melting with this stuff that comes out of me when I am wild for you. It comes when your fingers touch me, and it comes when your splendid wand is between my legs or even comes near this wet, hot place. Yes, I'm hot, I'm throbbing, my fingers are rubbing and pressing there, but I want you to do it. Is yours big and hard and straight as you read this? I want to take it in my hand! Oh, take down your clothes, my man, touch and rub yourself and make believe it is my hand there as my hand so often was. I am making believe that this is your hand here between my legs.

I could not write for a while; I had to sit and press and rub myself with both hands as I saw you take out that great thing of yours and begin to play with it in your hands. Do you know what I want to do? I want to kneel down and take that thing in my hands and put it in my mouth and suck it and suck it and suck it!

Toss me up and down, there on your legs, astride you! Jounce me and let me feel that big wand poking and jerking about inside of me! I love that feeling! Oh, I want you, I want you to fill me, to flood me, to make me mad with the joy you give me!

I had to get up and walk about the room a little. If you were to look in here, you would see strange sights! First, this woman sits at the desk and writes fiercely; then she gets up and takes off her robe and walks around. You can see her naked body, her legs in silk stockings to just above the knees, but nothing over the curly hair of her sex, nothing covering her breasts, and if you came to her you could put your arms around her naked hips and waist. Her hair is all loose and hanging, and she would so gladly run, naked and laughing and happy, into your arms!

Several minutes have elapsed, beloved. I must finish this letter somehow. I am trembling all over. Do you know why? Because my madness overcame me, my desire too great, the tickling, throbbing, itching ache of it was more than I could stand and I made it come to its climax. Yes, I went and threw myself face down on the sofa, my hands between my legs, and I held two fingers straight and put them inside me, and then I tossed and heaved and rubbed and jerked about with my legs wide apart, and I thought of you and twitched my fingers in and out and the feeling got bigger and bigger and suddenly I just seemed to open up inside as if to take you in and…I came!

The thrills are still running over me. Before I let you go, I want you to come. You must! See, I am stark naked! Shall I make you come by sucking it? Do you want your wicked, naked girl to take it in her mouth and suck it? That's what I'm doing in imagination! I am lying all curled up on you; you are lying flat in bed! How it sticks up! My lips touch it, my tongue touches it. I like the feel of it against my lips. I wet it all over with my tongue, and then I open my mouth and suck it in. You like that! I can tell by the way you twitch and move and by the happy sounds you make.

M-m-m-m! I love it! It's so big and so firm! Now I move my head up and down, sucking it in, letting it out, caressing it all over with my tongue, licking it, sucking it in again. At last! My man is coming, in my mouth! No, no! Don't take it away, I want it there in my mouth, I want to feel it stiffen and jerk! It trembles! Come, my lover, let me have it now! Come! Come! Spurt your bliss into my mouth! My naked body writhes! You are coming! Now!

I am your slave in love, yours, your sweetheart, not another's, body and soul of me yours alone, in grateful happiness....

CHAPTER THIRTEEN

XIII

Dear Reader: Isn't that a touching tale? I'll tell you there was quite a bit of touching going on between Betty, her father, and me each time he told it. I hope you found it touching as well.

Without a doubt, that summer in the country was the culmination of my education in pleasure. All that I have experienced since pales by comparison to those sweet days of youthful vigor. Peter, for that was the Christian name of Betty's father, was the last to introduce me to new sensual delights. He took me in hand, as it were, he had so many others and showed me how satisfying life can be.

Here, finally, is a tale he told me of his experience the prior summer. I was later privileged to meet Alice and Gladys and Bill, and we all spent many enjoyable languid summer hours together. But here is Peter's tale of how it all began.

Last summer Alice and I were lovers. Alice was a young matron whose husband was much older than she and too busy to look after her as a healthy, normal young wife requires. I used to meet her at dances during the winter. She was a wonderful dancer and a little beauty. Needless to say, holding her in my arms while dancing made me wish to know her better. It was not long before little pressures of hands and arms were asking, and answering, unspoken questions. Without a word said, she let me know that some day she would consent to more.

Later, in the spring, we used to go walking together in the hills on pleasant afternoons. We would drive out into the country, hide the car somewhere on a quiet road, and wander off into the fresh green woods. We were fond of the secluded little glade we found one day, where we often reposed, sure of being undisturbed. But Alice, although generous with kisses and dear little caresses, entirely withheld herself otherwise, and I was much too fond of her, and too interested in discovering under what circumstances she would give herself, to press matters—beyond showing her clearly what I wanted. She quite understood. I knew it was only a matter of time before she would come to the point.

Her surrender came about under unusual circumstances. One lovely warm afternoon in May, we found our way to our little glade, but were surprised to find two other young lovers there before us. They, totally engaged in each other, did not hear us. We stealthily withdrew a short distance and sat down in a little pocket among the bushes to see what would happen. Alice, I could easily see, was very much excited and interested.

The girl was lying on her back in the shade of a tree. The man lay beside her and their lips were together. We could hear the indistinct murmur of their voices. Hunched up as we two were in our little hiding place, quite close together, I did not find it hard, nor think it wrong, to put my lips to Alice's. Alice clearly thought my conduct appropriate, for she returned my kiss with interest. The interest was paid in a tiny flutter of her tongue tip against my lips. Our kiss lasted quite a time.

When we looked again, the scene had changed somewhat. Alice gasped a little, as well she might. The lover was lying on one side, propped up on an elbow, and his free hand was disturbing the formerly smooth folds of his sweetheart's skirt. At the same time—to keep her distracted, perhaps—he was kissing her ardently. But his hand was under her skirt, and he'd pulled it up so we could see two shapely legs in pearl gray stockings. Two small feet in tiny slippers, very unsuitable for walking in the hills, were calmly crossed. The lover was caressing the silk-clad legs.

"Peter!" whispered Alice, remonstrating. For as she crouched there, somewhat curled up, one of her own very attractive legs lay outside the shelter of her skirt, and I had rested my hand on the silken fabric which covered it. But her attention must have been distracted too, for after that one remonstrance she leaned forward, her eyes intent on what she could see, while my hand continued to enjoy the delightful touch of silk stretched over a beautifully shaped leg.

I turned from admiring the contours of Alice's pretty leg to see what was happening to the pearl-gray ones. My hand, not being necessary for this, stayed where it was most comfortable. Those other legs had become most interesting. The skirt had been moved still higher, and the total length of the stockings was now visible. They ended not far above the knee, and I could see a great deal of two lovely thighs. The slippered feet now lay side by side, uncrossed, and the girl's arms, while her legs were being so lovingly caressed, were tight about the neck of her lover, holding his face to hers for kisses.

"Peter!" warned Alice again, in a tense whisper. Somehow, when I'd turned my eyes, my hand, being left to its own resources, had wandered a bit. In fact, it had strayed above the knee and was thrilling to the touch of soft, warm flesh. Alice stirred a bit, as if she were impatient with me, but it was satisfying to note that in doing so she thrust her leg still further out from under her skirt. Upon checking to see what results her movement might have had, I was overjoyed to see, right close at hand, a most enticing bit of white thigh. My hand made haste to embrace this opportunity, in fact to grasp at the unseen, as it felt its way, unhindered, to discover yet further pleasures.

"Peter, look!" whispered Alice. And we looked. Not fifteen feet away the other pair, unsuspecting still, pursued their own amusement: The girl had moved, her skirt was drawn up clear above her waist, and her hips and legs were entirely exposed. It was quite evident that the young lady wore no panties!

Her lover was sitting up, fussing with his own clothing, his eyes enjoying this vision of loveliness. Those two pretty legs were slightly parted now, and a dear little nest of hair was visible.

"Oh, Peter!" Alice gasped this time. For, as the man's clothing was unfastened, his sweetheart's hand reached out and took hold of something. He stretched out an instant and wriggled. One stockinged and red-gartered but otherwise bare leg came out of his trousers, then another bare leg, then the man's were placed between the woman's two; and, satisfied with this arrangement, the lover lay upon his sweetheart. His arms about her, hers about him, they began to move delicately as if rubbing on each other.

I found Alice's hand and, placing it in a certain position, showed her that I, too, had something which might be held, should her hand care to hold it. Indeed, soon she was holding it, and by playing with it—as if absentmindedly, you understand, and without taking her eyes from the scene before us—she brought me no little pleasure.

We could hear soft cooings and murmurs. Alice and I ceased to regard the others for a time. She moved closer into my arms, lay quite heavily there, in fact, and in so doing managed to arrange her clothing so that both her legs lay bare. To my real surprise, Alice, too, was guiltless of panties. Much reassured, I let my hands move freely over the delicious surfaces of her thighs and hips. Our lips were fast together, and now I learned how Alice could kiss when really interested. When my hand in its wanderings encountered certain soft curls, her lips and tongue assailed me with quite impetuous ardor.

But curiosity drew my eyes again to the other lovers. "Look, Alice!" I whispered to her, and as we looked, our hands became very busy and our eyes drank in a most lascivious sight. Side by side, now, the girl and the man were sitting, all outer clothing removed from their waists down, and the girl's blouse so opened that two dainty breasts hung out. The couple's lips were crushed together, while with their free hands they were playing with all their most delicious toys. The man's hand was moving between his sweetheart's parted legs; the girl's hand held something hard and stiff, which she manipulated gently.

"Oo-oo-oh!" gasped Alice, and fell to kissing me wildly. Needless to say, I kissed her wildly back. Her own hand held something hard and stiff, and her treatment of it was as skillful as it was delicious. My hand was between her lovely legs, and the manner in which she received its administrations showed that I had not forgotten how to play upon that organ which, if its keyboard be properly touched, causes a woman's body to reecho with all the greater and lesser harmonies.

Alice had at last abandoned her reserve, that withholding of herself. The discovery that she wore no panties made me suspect that she had intended from the start to give herself to me this day. But, as a matter of fact, I had no proof of any kind that she ever did wear panties, though I know that women at Alice's social level do ordinarily wear them. It was not, therefore, an altogether unnatural assumption that Alice ordinarily wore them, and that she did not do so this day because she intended to be more than ordinarily generous with me.

But I digress.... Alice, as I say, wore no panties, and her lovely naked thighs lay exposed to my hands and eyes. But her intentions were shown even more clearly by her conduct. Somehow, at some point, Alice had had experience. She had learned how to be charmingly wanton without being shameless. Her kisses were delights of art and skill, her movements were delicate yet effective, her grip was possessive without being painful, and her handling of what her fair hand held was, without being obtrusive, obviously intended to ultimately bring it between her legs.

"Peter, darling, look there!" Alice whispered between her kisses. Our lovers were at last in earnest, the man lying between the girl's legs, which were embracing and holding him while he moved with vigorous thrusts of his hips. "Peter!" cooed Alice, and "Alice!" I cooed back, and somehow her weight was upon me, her legs spread far apart, and she took me into herself.

In the course of time we sat up again and looked about. The other pair was sitting up, smiling in our direction. We were discovered! In our excitement we had moved so that our former shelter no longer concealed us. Strange to say, Alice did not seem concerned. Either she was accustomed to intimate acts of love with others about, which I really do not believe, or else she saw at once that we must make the best of the situation and, perhaps, profit by it. At any rate, she laughed quite gaily and stood up, shaking her skirt down to where it belonged. I stood up, too, but not so easily, as my trousers needed attention.

The other man called out, "What luck?"

"Fine," I answered, "a bull's eye!" Alice laughed again.

"Same here," responded the man, stepping nearer. "My name's Bill."

"Mine's Pete." And we shook hands. I presented Alice. She shook hands.

"Gladys," said Bill, "here's Pete and Alice. Come and get acquainted."

So, all introduced, we sat down. Bill and Gladys on either side of me, and Alice on the other side of Bill. We talked a bit, about everything but the events of the past hour. But after a time conversation waned. Bill was whispering to Alice, so I began to whisper to Gladys. What I said was of no importance to the other two, but it made Gladys laugh and her eyes shine. Furthermore, she put out her hand to see if what I had told her was true. Finding that it was, she seemed satisfied and lay back, smiling enticingly. Somehow I found that I was embracing her naked legs. Bill did not seem to mind, for he was doing the same to Alice!

It was most interesting to play this way with another man's sweetheart while the other man played with mine. There lay Alice, who had just given me a delicious half hour, doing the same for Bill—and believe me, I knew that Bill was lucky! And here lay Gladys, giving herself to my caresses as she had given herself to Bill not long before, and believe me, I soon knew that both Bill and I were lucky!

Gladys was not so voluptuously formed as Alice, but she knew her part and made every little movement have just the meaning that it should. Her little breasts were just as satisfactory to my hands and lips as Alice's fuller ones, and she responded just as delightfully to the skillful touch of my fingers. She was all woman, and ended by giving me a most glorious moment. Unless all familiar signs failed, Gladys received as much pleasure from my success as I did. Bill scored his second center shot almost at the same time. Both girls were flushed and radiant.

"Bill's bigger," confided Alice in a whisper as she nestled up against me, "but he hasn't your finesse, Peter, darling. But it was wonderful to get fucked twice!"

Gladys was whispering to Bill, and I heard his heavier voice whisper back, "I'm glad you liked it, honey!" So I guess Gladys had told him that she had been pleased.

Bill produced some liquid refreshment. I don't drink much, but it was good whiskey and the little glass went around among the four of us several times. The girls got just a little drunk, and I began to get interested. There's a certain something about taking a girl who is just a little bit intoxicated. Even the ardent ones become slightly more so, and the movements of a girl on the way to becoming drunk are most wanton.

It wasn't so very long before all of us, well stimulated, were huddled in an intimate group. The girls lay all over us two men and kissed us with wet lips. We fondled them and kissed them on the lips and on the nipples of their breasts, which they had left bare. The whiskey and the caresses soon had their natural effect.

"Pete, what's that?" Alice exclaimed, and made her eyes round with mocking amazement. For there it was again, as large as ever! "Gladys, see what I found, see what I found!" Alice called, as she unfastened my trousers and held her discovery in her hand. Gladys, without a word, unbuttoned Bill's trousers and took out what she found. No doubt about it, Bill's was bigger than mine! But the girls were each satisfied. I know we all four laughed at the picture: two very pretty girls, somewhat flushed with whiskey, their breasts bare, each sitting beside a recumbent man and holding a sceptre in her hand. We all took another drink.

Alice was getting very gay, and her kisses more and more amorous. She handled me lovingly and called me (or part of me) all sorts of amusing names. But I was surprised when, with a sudden change of position, she put her head down and began to kiss it. Gladys immediately did the same to Bill. We two men lay there a while, too contented to speak, and watched our sweethearts kiss and suck our cocks. Alice knew how to use her mouth; I have often wondered and never found out where and how she learned.

Neither man nor woman could stand that for long. Gladys curled around and got her leg over Bill, and Alice imitated her. I soon felt her, after a bit of rubbing, slide down upon me, hot and moist. The girls rode us so, and rubbed upon us as we bounced them with our knees and hips. They laughed and exclaimed and crooned and cooed, each holding the other's hand as they jounced about side by side on their willing mounts. Then both sat erect at almost the same moment, with that look of wondering delight that lovers love to see on their sweethearts' faces, and collapsed together, gasping, as Bill and I spurted for the third time!

It was now getting late. We all promised to meet again and went our separate ways. On the road home, leaning with her head against my shoulder as I drove, Alice made the most extraordinary remark I ever heard from her lips.

"Pete, I'm fucked to a frazzle!"

Perhaps she was then, but after a couple of cocktails and dinner at her house (her husband being away), she invited me to her room. There, on her own bed, and both of us, at her own request, all naked this time, I—well, the lady used the word first—fucked her again!

And as she lay there, stretched out so beautifully and happily naked when I kissed her good night and good-bye, she murmured tenderly, "Four times in one day, each time a wonder. But, Pete, darling, the last was the best!" And as I recall her naked body in my arms, its every fibre leaping in passionate desire, I think to myself that yes, it was the best.

The Masquerade Erotic Newsletter

◆◆◆◆◆◆◆◆◆◆◆◆◆◆◆◆◆◆◆◆◆◆

FICTION, ESSAYS, REVIEWS, PHOTOGRAPHY, INTERVIEWS, EXPOSÉS, AND MUCH MORE!

◆◆◆◆◆◆◆◆◆◆◆◆◆◆◆◆◆◆◆◆◆◆

"*The Masquerade Erotic Newsletter* presents some of the best articles on erotica, fetishes, sex clubs, the politics of porn and every conceivable issue of sex and sexuality." —*Factsheet Five*

"I received the new issue of the newsletter;—it looks better and better."

—Michael Perkins

"It's always a treat to see a copy of *The Masquerade Erotic Newsletter*, for it brings a sophisticated and unexpected point of view to bear on the world of erotica, and does this with intelligence, tolerance, and compassion." —Martin Shepard, co-publisher, The Permanent Press

"Fun articles on writing porn and about the peep shows, great for those of us who will probably never step onto a strip stage or behind the glass of a booth, but love to hear about it, wicked little voyeurs that we all are, hm? Yes indeed...." —MT, California

"Many thanks for your newsletter with essays on various forms of eroticism. Especially enjoyed your new Masquerade collections of books dealing with gay sex." —GF, Maine

"... a professional, insider's look at the world of erotica ..."

—*SCREW*

"I recently received a copy of *The Masquerade Erotic Newsletter*. I found it to be quite informative and interesting. The intelligent writing and choice of subject matter are refreshing and stimulating. You are to be congratulated for a publication that looks at different forms of eroticism without leering or smirking." —DP, Connecticut

"Thanks for sending the books and the two latest issues of *The Masquerade Erotic Newsletter*. Provocative reading, I must say."

—RH, Washington

◆◆◆◆◆◆◆◆◆◆◆◆◆◆◆◆◆◆◆◆◆◆

EROTIC *PLAYGIRL* ROMANCES $4.95

LOVE & SURRENDER

Marlene Darcy

"Madeline saw Harry looking at her legs and she blushed as she remembered what he wanted to do.... She casually pulled the skirt of her dress back to uncover her knees and the lower part of her thighs. What did he want now? Did he want more? She tugged at her skirt again, pulled it back far enough so almost all of her thighs were exposed...." **3082-2**

THE COMPLETE *PLAYGIRL* FANTASIES

The best women's fantasies are collected here, fresh from the pages of *Playgirl*. These knockouts from the infamous "Reader's Fantasy Forum" prove, once again, that truth can indeed be hotter, wilder, and *better* than fiction. **3075-X**

CHARLOTTE ROSE

THE DOCTOR IS IN

From the author of the acclaimed ***Women at Work*** comes a delectable trio of fanastasies inspired by one of life's most intimate relationships. Charlotte Rose once again writes about women's forbidden desires, this time from the patient's point of view. Fast becoming a favorite among women everywhere for her frank and gutsy style, Rose is in rare form in this steamy ode to the medical profession. Open and say 'Aaaahhhh...!' **195-0**

WOMEN AT WORK

Hot, uninhibited stories devoted to the working woman! From a lonesome cowgirl to a supercharged public relations exec, these uncontrollable women know how to let off steam after a tough day on the job. Career pursuits pale beside their devotion to less professional pleasures, as each proves that "moonlighting" is often the best job of all! A wildly popular and critically acclaimed title, that includes "A Cowgirl's Passion," ranked #1 on Dr. Ruth's list of favorite erotic stories for women! **3088-1**

GWYNETH JAMES

FOR A PIRATE'S KISS

The place: Port Royal, Jamaica, in the exotic Caribbean. The year: 1665, a time of chivalry, swashbuckling, and civilized barbarism. One woman learns her way about the rollicking seaport town, largely through visiting the beds of Port Royal's most colorful men. **156-X**

DREAM CRUISE

Angelia has it all—a brilliant career and a beautiful face to match. But she longs to kick up her high heels and have some fun, so she takes an island vacation and vows to leave her sexual inhibitions behind. From the moment her plane takes off, she finds herself in one hot and steamy encounter after another, and her horny holiday doesn't end on Monday morning! **3045-0**

SYDNEY ST. JAMES

THE HIGHWAYWOMAN

A young filmmaker making a documentary about the life of the notorious English highwaywoman, Bess Ambrose, becomes obseesed with her mysterious subject. It seems that Bess touched more than the hearts of the nobles she robbed and plundered the treasures of every man and maiden she met on the way. **174-8**

GARDEN OF DELIGHT

A vivid account of sexual awakening that follows an innocent but insatiably curious young woman's journey from the furtive, forbidden joys of dormitory life to the unabashed carnality of the wild world. Pretty Pauline blossoms with each new experiment in the sensual arts. **3058-X**

THE LOVING DOMINANT

Everything you need to know about an infamous sexual variation—and an unspoken type of love. Mentor—a longtime player in the dominance/submission scene—guides readers through this rarely seen world, and offers clear-eyed advice guaranteed to enlighten the most jaded erotic explorers. Mentor reveals the too-often hidden basis of the D/S relationship: the care, trust and love between partners. 218-3

GRANT ANTREWS

SUBMISSIONS

Another stunning, sensitive tale from the author of ***My Darling Dominatrix***. Once again, Antrews portrays the very special elements of the dominant/submissive relationship with restraint—this time with the story of a lonely man, a winning lottery ticket, and a demanding dominatrix. Grant Antrews is one of erotica's most discerning writers; never leering, he explores his lovers' exotic world and the remarkable bonds it engenders. 207-8

MY DARLING DOMINATRIX

A remarkable and uncompromising debut novel from major talent. When a man and a woman fall in love it's supposed to be simple, uncomplicated, easy—unless that woman happens to be a dominatrix. Curiosity gives way to unblushing desire in this story of one man's awakening to the joys to be experienced as the willing slave of a powerful woman. This unpretentious love story captures the richness and depth of this very special kind of love. 3055-5

SARA ADAMSON

THE SLAVE

The second volume in the astonishing "Marketplace" trilogy. ***The Slave*** covers the experience of one exceptionally talented submissive who longs to join the ranks of those who have proven themselves worthy of entry into the Marketplace. But the price, while delicious, is staggeringly high.... Adamson's plot thickens, as her trilogy moves to a mindblowing conclusion in the forthcoming ***The Trainer***. 173-X

THE MARKETPLACE

"Merchandise does not come easily to the Marketplace.... They haunt the clubs and the organizations, their need so real and desperate that they exude sensual tension when they glide through the crowds. Some of them are so ripe that they intimidate the poseurs, the weekend sadists and the furtive dilettantes who are so endemic to that world. And they never stop asking where we may be found...." A compelling tale of the ultimate training academy, where only the finest are accepted and trained for service beyond their wildest dreams 3096-2

THE CATALYST

After viewing a controversial, explicitly kinky film full of images of bondage and submission, several audience members find themselves deeply moved by the erotic suggestions they've seen on the screen. Each inspired coupling explores their every imagined extreme, as long-denied urges explode! 3015-6/$4.95

DAVID AARON CLARK

SISTER RADIANCE

From the author of the acclaimed ***The Wet Forever***, comes a chronicle of obsession, rife with Clark's trademark vivisections of contemporary desires, sacred and profane. The vicissitudes of lust and romance are examined against a backdrop of urban decay and shallow fashionability in this testament to the allure—and inevitability—of the forbidden. 215-9

THE WET FOREVER

The story of Janus and Madchen, a small-time hood and a beautiful sex worker, ***The Wet Forever*** examines themes of loyalty, sacrifice, redemption and obsession amidst Manhattan's sex parlors and underground S/M clubs. Its combination of sex and suspense makes ***The Wet Forever*** singular, uncompromising, and strangely arousing—and led Terence Sellers to proclaim it "evocative and poetic." **117-9**

ALICE JOANOU

TOURNIQUET

A brand new collection of stories and effusions from the pen of one our most dazzling young writers. Strange tales abound, from the story of the mysterious and cruel Cybele, to an encounter with the sadistic entertainment of a bizarre after-hours cafe. By turns lush and austere, Joanou's intoxicating command of language and image makes ***Tourniquet*** a sumptuous feast for all the senses. Strong stuff from a writer at the beginning of her career. **3060-1**

CANNIBAL FLOWER

"She is waiting in her darkened bedroom, as she has waited throughout history, to seduce the men who are foolish enough to be blinded by her irresistible charms. She is Salome, Lucrezia Borgia, Delilah—endlessly alluring, the fulfillment of your every desire.... She is the goddess of sexuality, and ***Cannibal Flower*** is her haunting siren song."—Michael Perkins **$4.95/72-6**

MICHAEL PERKINS

EVIL COMPANIONS

A handsome edition of this cult classic that includes a new preface by Samuel R. Delany on the creation of this brutal novel. Set in New York City during the tumultuous waning years of the Sixties, ***Evil Companions*** has been hailed as "a frightening classic." A young couple explore the nether reaches of the erotic unconscious in a shocking confrontation with the extremes of passion. This acclaimed novel, out of print for years, returns with a special Afterword by the author. **3067-9**

AN ANTHOLOGY OF CLASSIC ANONYMOUS EROTIC WRITING

Michael Perkins, acclaimed authority on erotic literature, has collected the very best passages from the world's erotic writing—especially for Rhinoc***eros*** readers. "Anonymous" is one of the most infamous bylines in publishing history—and these steamy excerpts show why! Masterpieces of an underground genre. **140-3**

THE SECRET RECORD: Modern Erotic Literature

Michael Perkins, a renowned author and critic of sexually explicit fiction, surveys the field with authority and unique insight. Updated and revised to include the latest trends, tastes, and developments in this much-misunderstood and maligned genre. An important volume for every erotic reader and fan of high quality adult fiction, ***The Secret Record*** is finally back in print, and ready to take on erotica's toughest opponents. **3039-3**

HELEN HENLEY

ENTER WITH TRUMPETS

Helen Henley was told that woman just don't write about sex—much less the taboos she was so interested in exploring. So Henley did it alone, flying in the face of "tradition" by producing ***Enter With Trumpets***, a touching tale of arousal and devotion in one couple's kinky relationship. ***Enter With Trumpets*** proves what Henley knew all along: that the expression of human desire acknowledges no rules but its own. **197-7**

TUPPY OWENS

SENSATIONS

A piece of porn history. Tuppy Owens tells the unexpurgated story of the making of *Sensations*—the first big-budget sex flick. Originally commissioned to appear in book form after the release of the film in 1975, ***Sensations*** is finally released under Masquerade's stylish Rhino*ceros* imprint. A document from a more reckless, bygone time! **3081-4**

DANIEL VIAN

ILLUSIONS

Two disturbing tales of danger and desire on the eve of WWII. From private homes to lurid cafés to decaying streets, passion is explored, exposed, and placed in stark contrast to the brutal violence of the time. ***Illusions*** peels the frightened mask from the face of desire, and studies its changing features under the dim lights of a lonely Berlin evening. Two unforgettable and evocative stories return to print in one special volume. **3074-1**

PERSUASIONS

"The stockings are drawn tight by the suspender belt, tight enough to be stretched to the limit just above the middle part of her thighs..." A double novel, including the classics ***Adagio*** and ***Gabriela and the General***, this volume traces desire around the globe. International lust! **183-7**

LIESEL KULIG

LOVE IN WARTIME

An uncompromising look at the politcs, perils and pleasures of sexual power. Madeleine knew that the handsome SS officer was a dangerous man. But she was just a cabaret singer in Nazi-occupied Paris, trying to survive in a perilous time. When Josef fell in love with her, he discovered that a beautiful and amoral woman can sometimes be wildly dangerous. **3044-X**

MASQUERADE BOOKS $4.95

CHARLEY'S GAME *Bren Flemming*

Charley's a no-nonsense private detective facing the fight of her life. A rich woman's gullible daughter has run off with one of the toughest leather dykes in town—and Charley's hired to lure the girl back. One by one, wise and wicked women ensnare one another in their lusty nets—until the final explosive encounter! 221-3

ANDREA AT THE CENTER *J.P. Kansas*

"You're going to be part of a special community for a few months. You'll be treated well here at the center. It's going to be the most enlightening experience of your life. When it's over, you'll be returned to where you come from." Kidnapped! Lithe and lovely young Andrea is, without warning, whisked away to a distant retreat. Gradually, she is introduced to the ways of the Center, and soon becomes quite friendly with its other inhabitants—all of whom are learning to abandon all restraint in their pursuit of the deepest sexual satisfaction. 206-X

ASK ISADORA *Isadora Alman*

An essential volume, collecting six years' worth of Isadora Alman's syndicated columns on sex and relationships. Alman's been called a "hip Dr. Ruth," and a "sexy Dear Abby," based upon the wit and pertinence of her advice. Today's world is more perplexing than ever—and Isadora Alman is just the expert to help untangle the most personal of knots. 61-0

LESSONS AND LOVERS *Elaine Platero*

"Hettie felt like a kind of sex-doll for the other two, a living breathing female body to demonstrate the responses and vulnerabilities of womankind to a young man who was hungry for knowledge...." When a repressed widow, her all-too-willing manservant, a voluptuous doctor and an anxious neophyte take a country weekend together, crucial lessons are learned by all! 196-9

PROTESTS, PLEASURES AND RAPTURES *Anonymous*

Invited for an allegedly quiet weekend at a country Vicarage, a young woman is stunned to find herself surrounded by shocking acts of sexual sadism. Her curiosity is piqued, and she begins to explore her own capacities for cruelty—leading to a search for an appropriately punishable partner. 204-3

THE SLAVES OF SHOANNA *Mercedes Kelly*

Shoanna, the cruel and magnificent, takes four maidens under her wing—and teaches them the ins and outs of pleasure and discipline. The four are trained in every imaginable way: from simple fleshly joys to techniques for the handling of unimaginable instruments. Slutty students go straight to the head of the class! 164-0

CONFESSIONS OF A CONCUBINE *Anonymous*

What *really* happens behind the plush walls of the harem? An inexperienced woman, captured and sentenced to service the royal pleasure, tells all in an outrageously unrestrained memoir. No affairs of state could match the passions of a young woman learning to relish a life of ceaseless sexual servitude. 154-3

THE DARKER PASSIONS: *DRACULA* *Amarantha Knight*

From the realm of legend comes the grand beast of eros, the famed and dreaded defiler of innocence. His name is Dracula, and no virgin is protected from his unspeakable ravishments. One by one he brings his victims to the ecstasy that will make them his—forever. A classic fiend recast as the ultimate voluptuary. 147-0

MASTER OF TIMBERLAND *Sara H. French*

Luscious slaves serve randy tourists in this ultimate vacation paradise. Only the most willing and voluptuous are admitted, and trained to accomodate every whim of the horny vacationers—all of whom choose their slaves with discretion, and rule with an iron fist. 3059-8

MASQUERADE BOOKS $4.95

HARRIET DAIMLER

DARLING • INNOCENCE

In *Darling*, a virgin is raped by a mugger. Driven by her urge for revenge, she searches New York for him in a furious sexual hunt that leads to rape and murder. In ***Innocence***, a young invalid determines to experience sex through her voluptuous nurse. Two critically acclaimed novels in one volume make this a must! **3047-4**

THE PLEASURE THIEVES

They are the Pleasure Thieves, two lusty and larcenous men whose sexually preoccupied targets are set up by luscious Carol Stoddard. She forms an ultra-hot sexual threesome with them, trying every combination from two-on-ones to daisy chains—but always on the sly, because pleasures are even sweeter when they're stolen! **036-X**

AKBAR DEL PIOMBO

SKIRTS

Randy Mr. Edward Champdick enters high society—and a whole lot more—in his quest for ultimate satisfaction. For it seems that once Mr. Champdick rises to the occasion, nothing can bring him down. Nothing, that is, except indiscriminate gratification under the nearest skirt. Rampant ravishment! **115-2**

DUKE COSIMO

A kinky, lighthearted romp played out against the boudoirs, bathrooms and ballrooms of the European nobility, who seem to do nothing all day except each other. The lurid lifestyles of the rich and licentious are revelaed in all their glory. A must for all fans of creative decadence and lust! **3052-0**

A CRUMBLING FAÇADE

The return of that incorrigible rogue, Henry Pike,who continues his pursuit of sex, fair or otherwise, in the most elegant homes of the most irreproachable and debauched aristocrats. No one can resist the irrespressible Pike—especially when this freewheeling fornicator's on the prowl. **3043-1**

PAULA

"How bad do you want me?" she asked, her voice husky, breathy. I shrank back, for my desire for her was swelling to unspeakable proportions. "Turn around," she said, and I obeyed....This canny seductress tests the mettle of every man who comes under her spell—and every man does! One of erotica's most popular vixens. **3036-9**

ROBERT DESMOND

PROFESSIONAL CHARMER

A gigolo lives a parasitical life of luxury by providing his sexual services to the rich and bored. Traveling in the most exclusive circles, this gun-for-hire will gratify the lewdest and most vulgar sexual cravings. Every exploit is described in lurid detail in this story of a prostitute's progress! **3003-2**

THE SWEETEST FRUIT

Connie is determined to seduce and destroy Father Chadcrof. She corrupts the priest into forsaking all that he holds sacred, destroys his peaceful parish, and slyly manipulates him with her smoldering looks and hypnotic aura. **95-5**

MICHAEL DRAX

SILK AND STEEL

"He stood tall and strong in the shadows of her room... Akemi knew what he was there for. He let his robe fall to the floor. She could offer no resistance as the shadowy figure knelt before her, gazing down upon her. Why would she resist? This was what she wanted all along...." **3032-6**

MASQUERADE BOOKS $4.95

EROTOMANIA

The bible of female sexual perversion! It's all here, everything you ever wanted to know about kinky women past and present. From simple nymphomania to the most outrageous fetishism, all secrets are revealed in this look into the forbidden rooms of feminine desire. **128-4**

AN ALIZARIN LAKE READER

A selection of wicked musings from the pen of Masquerade's perennially popular author. It's all here: ***Business as Usual, The Erotic Adventures of Harry Temple, Festival of Venus,*** the mysterious ***Instruments of the Passion***, the devilish ***Miss High Heels***—and more. **106-3**

SEX ON DOCTOR'S ORDERS

A chronicle of selfless devotion to mankind! Beth, a nubile young nurse, uses her considerable skills to further science by offering incomparable and insatiable assistance in the gathering of important specimens. No man leaves Nurse Beth's station without surrendering exactly what she needs—because everyone is covered under naughty Nurse Beth's comprehensive plan for Humpy Healthcare! **3092-X**

MISS HIGH HEELS

It was a delightful punishment few men dared to dream of. Who could have predicted how far it would go? Forced by his sisters to dress and behave like a proper lady, Dennis Beryl finds he enjoys life as Denise much more! Soon Dennis discovers the sizzling delights that await good, bad girls. **3066-0**

THE INSTRUMENTS OF THE PASSION

All that remains is the diary of a young initiate, detailing the twisted rituals of a mysterious cult institution known only as "Rossiter." Behind sinister walls, a beautiful young woman performs an unending drama of pain and humiliation. To what lengths will her aberrant passion drive her? **3010-5**

CLARA

The death of a beautiful, aristocratic woman leads her old boyfriend on an harrowing journey. His search uncovers a woman on a quest for deeper and more unusual sensations, each more shocking then the one before. **80-7**

FESTIVAL OF VENUS

Brigeen Mooney fled her home in the west of Ireland to avoid being forced into a nunnery. But her refuge in Dublin turned out to be dedicated to a different religion. The women she met there belonged to the Old Religion, devoted to sex and sacrifices. Sex ceremonies of pagan gods! **37-8**

PAUL LITTLE

TUTORED IN LUST

This tale of the initiation and instruction of a carnal college co-ed and her fellow students unlocks the sex secrets of the classroom. Books take a back seat to secret societies and their bizarre ceremonies in this story of students with an unquenchable thirst for knowledge! **78-5**

DANGEROUS LESSONS

A compendium of corporeal punishment from the twisted mind of bestselling Paul Little. Incredibly arousing morsels abound: ***Tears of the Inquisition, Lust of the Cossacks, Poor Darlings, Captive Maidens, Slave Island,*** even the scandalous ***The Metamorphosis of Lisette Joyaux***. A rump-roasting roundup of Little's wicked best. **32/7**

THE LUSTFUL TURK

The majestic ruler of Algiers and a modest English virgin face off—to their mutual delight. Emily Bartow is initially horrified by the unrelenting sexual tortures to be endured under the powerful Turk's hand. But soon she comes to crave her debasement—even when it appears that his twisted desires know no bounds! **163-2**

MASQUERADE BOOKS $4.95

THE STORY OF MONIQUE

Between the lesbians who came to Sonia's parties, and the convent where nuns and monks fell upon each other in orgiastic madness, Monique soon discovered within herself an endless appetite for sex! Luckily, Monique would never find that appetite unsatisfied—thanks to an insatiable circle of acquaintances. **42-4**

THE FURTHER ADVENTURES OF MADELEINE

"What mortal pen can describe these driven orgasmic transports?" writes Madeleine as she explores Paris' sexual underground. She discovers that the finest clothes may cover the most twisted personalities of all! **04-1**

THE AMERICAN COLLECTION

LUST *Palmiro Vicarion*

A wealthy and powerful man of leisure recounts his rise up the corporate ladder and his corresponding descent into debauchery. Adventure and political intrigue provide a stimulating backdrop for this tale of a classic scoundrel with an uncurbed appetite for sexual power! **82-3**

WAYWARD *Peter Jason*

A mysterious countess hires a tour bus for an unusual vacation. Traveling through Europe's most notorious cities, she picks up friends, lovers, and acquaintances from every walk of life in pursuit of unbridled sensual pleasure. Countless orgies, outrageous acts, and endless deviation! **3004-0**

LOVE'S ILLUSION

Elizabeth Renard yearned for the body of Dan Harrington. Then she discovers Harrington's secret weakness: a need to be humiliated and punished. She makes him her slave, and together they commence a journey into depravity that leaves nothing to the imagination—*nothing!* **100-4**

THE RELUCTANT CAPTIVE

Sarah is kidnapped by ruthless outlaws who kill her husband and burn their prosperous ranch. Her journey takes her from the bordellos of the Wild West to the bedrooms of Boston, until she is bought at last by a mysterious stranger from her past. **3022-9**

LUSTY LESSONS

The priveleged and attractive David Elston had everything except the ability to fulfill the unrelenting demands of his passion. His efforts end in failure until he meets a stranger who takes him to a forbidden land of pleasure. **31-9**

DANCE HALL GIRLS

The dance hall studio in Modesto was ruthless trap for men and women of all ages. They learned to dance under the tutelage of sexual professionals. So grateful were they for the attention, they opened their hearts and their wallets. Scandalous sexual slavery! **44-0**

SAMUEL R. DELANY

THE MAD MAN

For his thesis, graduate student John Marr researches the life and work of the brilliant Timothy Hasler: a philosopher whose career was cut tragically short over a decade earlier. Marr encounters numerous obstacles, as other researchers turn up evidence of Hasler's personal life that is deemed simply too unpleasant. On another front, Marr finds himself increasingly drawn toward more shocking, depraved sexual entaglements with the homeless men of his neighborhood, until it begins to seem that Hasler's death might hold some key to his own life as a gay man in the age of AIDS.

This new novel by Samuel R. Delany not only expands the parameters of what he has given us in the past, but fuses together two seemingly disparate genres of writing and comes up with something which is not comparable to any existing text of which I am aware.... What Delany has done here is take the ideas of Marquis de Sade one step further, by filtering extreme and obsessive sexual behavior through the sieve of post-modern experience....
—Lambda Book Report

The latest novel from Hugo- and Nebula-winning science fiction writer and critic Delany... reads like a pornographic reflection of Peter Ackroyd's Chatterton *or A.S. Byatt's* Possession.... *The pornographic element... becomes more than simple shock or titillation, though, as Delany develops an insightful dichotomy between [his protagonist]'s two worlds: the one of cerebral philosophy and dry academia, the other of heedless, 'impersonal' obsessive sexual extremism. When these worlds finally collide ... the novel achieves a surprisingly satisfying resolution....—Publishers Weekly*

hardcover **193-4/$23.95**

THE MOTION OF LIGHT IN WATER

"*A very moving, intensely fascinating literary biography from an extraordinary writer. Thoroughly admirable candor and luminous stylistic precision; the artist as a young man and a memorable picture of an age.*" —William Gibson

"*A remarkably candid and revealing...study of an extraordinary and extraordinarily appealing human being, and a fascinating...account of the early days of a significant science fiction writer's career.*" —Robert Silverberg

The first unexpurgated American edition of award-winning author Samuel R. Delany's riveting autobiography covers the early years of one of science fiction's most important voices. Beginning with his marriage to the young, remarkably gifted poet Marilyn Hacker, Delany paints a vivid and compelling picture of New York's East Village in the early '60s—a time of unprecedented social change and transformation. Startling and revealing, ***The Motion of Light in Water*** traces the roots of one of America's most innovative writers. ***133-0***

LUCY TAYLOR

UNNATURAL ACTS

A remarkable debut volume from a provocative writer. ***Unnatural Acts*** plunges deep into the dark side of the psyche, far past all pleasantries and prohibitions, and brings to life a disturbing vision of erotic horror. Unrelenting angels and hungry gods play with souls and bodies in Taylor's murky cosmos: where heaven and hell are merely differences of perspective; where redemption and damnation lie behind the same shocking acts. ***181-0***

ROBERT PATRICK

TEMPLE SLAVE

...you must read this book. It draws such a tragic, and, in a way, noble portrait of Mr. Buono: It leads the reader, almost against his will, into a deep sympathy with this strange man who tried to comfort, to encourage and to feed both the worthy and the worthless... It is impossible not to mourn for this man—impossible not to praise this book. —Quentin Crisp

This is nothing less than the secret history of the most theatrical of theaters, the most bohemian of Americans and the most knowing of queens. Patrick writes with a lush and witty abandon, as if this departure from the crafting of plays has energized him. ***Temple Slave*** *is also one of the best ways to learn what it was like to be fabulous, gay, theatrical and loved in a time at once more and less dangerous to gay life than our own.—Genre*

Temple Slave tells the story of the Espresso Buono—the archetypal alternative performance space—and the wildly talented misfits who called it home in the early 60s. The Buono became the birthplace of a new underground theater—and the personal and social consciousness that would lead to Stonewall and the modern gay and lesbian movement. ***Temple Slave*** is a kaleidoscopic page from gay history—a riotous tour de force peppered with the verbal fireworks and shrewd insight that are the hallmark of Robert Patrick's work. **191-8**

KATHLEEN K.

SWEET TALKERS

Kathleen K. is a professional, in the finest sense of the word. She takes her work seriously, always approaching it with diligence, imagination and backbone; an exceptional judge of character, she manages both customers and employees with a flair that has made her business a success. But many people would dismiss Kathleen's achievements, falling as they do, outside mainstream corporate America.

Here, for the first time, is the story behind the provocative advertisements and 970 prefixes. Kathleen K. opens up her diary for a rare peek at the day-to-day life of a phone sex operator—and reveals a number of secrets and surprises. Because far from being a sleazy, underground scam, the service Kathleen provides often speaks to the lives of its customers with a directness and compassion they receive nowhere else. ***192-6***

DAVID MELTZER

THE AGENCY TRILOGY

With the Essex House edition of ***The Agency*** in 1968, the highly regarded poet David Meltzer took America on a trip into a hell of unbridled sexuality. The story of a supersecret, Orwellian sexual network, ***The Agency*** explored issues of erotic dominance and submission with an immediacy and frankness previously unheard of in American literature, as well as presenting a vision of an America consumed and dehumanised by a lust for power. This landmark novel was followed by ***The Agent***, and ***How Many Blocks in the Pile?***—taken with ***The Agency,*** they confirm Meltzer's position as one of America's early masters of the erotic genre.

...'The Agency' is clearly Meltzer's paradigm of society; a mindless machine of which we are all 'agents' including those whom the machine supposedly serves.... —Norman Spinrad

216-7

RICHARD KASAK BOOKS $12.95

CARO SOLES

MELTDOWN!

An Anthology of Erotic Science Fiction and Dark Fantasy for Gay Men

Editor Caro Soles has put together one of the most explosive, mind-bending collections of gay erotic writing ever published. ***Meltdown!*** contains the very best examples of this increasingly popular sub-genre: stories meant to shock and delight, to send a shiver down the spine and start a fire down below. An extraordinary volume, ***Meltdown!*** presents both new voices and provocative pieces by world-famous writers Edmund White and Samuel R. Delany. ***203-5***

BIZARRE SEX

BIZARRE SEX AND OTHER CRIMES OF PASSION

Edited by Stan Tal

Stan Tal, editor of *Bizarre Sex*, Canada's boldest fiction publication, has culled the very best stories that have crossed his desk—and now unleashes them on the reading public in ***Bizarre Sex and Other Crimes of Passion***. Over twenty small masterpieces of erotic shock make this one of the year's most unexpectedly alluring anthologies. Including such masters of erotic horror and fantasy as Edward Lee, Lucy Taylor, Nancy Kilpatrick and Caro Soles, ***Bizarre Sex and Other Crimes of Passion***, is a treasure-trove of arousing chills. ***213-2***

PAT CALIFIA

SENSUOUS MAGIC

> ***Sensuous Magic*** *is clear, succinct and engaging even for the reader for whom S/M isn't the sexual behavior of choice.... Califia's prose is soothing, informative and non-judgemental—she both instructs her reader and explores the territory for them.... When she is writing about the dynamics of sex and the technical aspects of it, Califia is the Dr. Ruth of the alternative sexuality set....*
>
> *—Lambda Book Report*

> *Don't take a dangerous trip into the unknown—buy this book and know where you're going!* *—SKIN TWO*

> *Finally, a "how to" sex manual that doesn't involve new age mumbo jumbo or "tricks" that require the agility of a Flying Wallenda.... Califia's strength as a writer lies in her ability to relay information without sounding condescending. If you don't understand a word or concept... chances are it's defined in the handy dictionary in the back....* *—Futuresex*

Renowned erotic pioneer Pat Califia provides this honest, unpretentious peek behind the mask of dominant/submissive sexuality—an adventurous adult world of pleasure too often obscured by ignorance and fear. Califia demystifies "the scene" for the novice, explaining the terminology and technique behind many misunderstood sexual practices The adventurous (or just plain curious) lover won't want to miss this ultimate "how to" volume. ***131-4***

SKIN TWO

THE BEST OF *SKIN TWO* *Edited by Tim Woodward*

For over a decade, *Skin Two* has served as the bible of the international fetish community. A groundbreaking journal from the crossroads of sexuality, fashion, and art, *Skin Two* specializes in provocative, challenging essays by the finest writers working in the "radical sex" scene. Collected here, for the first time, are the articles and interviews that have established the magazine's singular reputation. Including interviews with cult figures Tim Burton, Clive Barker and Jean Paul Gaultier. ***130-6***

GAUNTLET

THE BEST OF *GAUNTLET*

Edited by Barry Hoffman

No material, no opinion is taboo enough to violate Gauntlet*'s purpose of 'exploring the limits of free expression'—airing all views in the name of the First Amendment.* —Associated Press

Dedicated to "exploring the limits of free expression," *Gauntlet* has, with its semi-annual issues, taken on such explosive topics as race, pornography, political correctness, and media manipulation—always publishing the widest possible range of opinions. Only in *Gauntlet* might one expect to encounter Phyllis Schafley *and* Annie Sprinkle, Stephen King *and* Madonna—often within pages of one another. The very best, most provocative articles have been gathered by editor-in-chief Barry Hoffman, to make ***The Best of Gauntlet*** a most provocative exploration of American society's limits. ***202-7***

JOHN PRESTON

MY LIFE AS A PORNOGRAPHER

The erotic nonfiction of John Preston. Includes the title essay, given as the John Pearson Perry Lecture at Harvard University, and the legendary "Good-Bye to Sally Gearhart," and many other provocative writings.

*...essential and enlightening...His sex-positive stand on safer-sex education as the only truly effective AIDS-prevention strategy will certainly not win him any conservative converts, but AIDS activists will be shouting their assent.... [**My Life as a Pornographer**] is a bridge from the sexually liberated 1970s to the more cautious 1990s, and Preston has walked much of that way as a standard-bearer to the cause for equal rights.... —Library Journal*

*Preston's a model essayist; he writes pellucid prose in a voice that, like Samuel Johnson's, combines authority with entertainment.... **My Life as a Pornographer**...is not pornography, but rather reflections upon the writing and production of it. Preston ranges from really superb journalism of his interviews with denizens of the S/M demi-mond, particularly a superb portrait of a Colt model Preston calls "Joe" to a brilliant analysis of the "theater" of the New York sex club, The Mineshaft.... In a deeply sex-phobic world, Preston has never shied away from a vision of the redemptive potential of the erotic drive. Better than perhaps anyone in our community, Preston knows how physical joy can bridge differences and make us well.*

—Lambda Book Report

135-7

HUSTLING:

A GENTLEMAN'S GUIDE TO THE FINE ART OF HOMOSEXUAL PROSTITUTION

John Preston solicited the advice of "working boys" from across the country in his effort to produce the ultimate guide to the hustler's world. ***Hustling*** covers every practical aspect of the business, from clientele and payment options to "specialties," sidelines and drawbacks. No stone is left unturned in this guidebook to the ins and outs of this much-mythologized trade.

...valuable insights to many aspects of the world of gay male prostitution. Throughout the book, Preston uses materials gathered from interviews and letters from former and active hustlers, as well as insights gleaned from his own experience as a hustler.... Preston does fulfill his desire to entertain as well as educate. —Lambda Book Report

137-3

THE MASQUERADE EROTIC LIBRARY

ADAM&EVE	93-9	$4.95
AFFINITIES	3113-6	$4.95
ALIZARIN LAKE READER, AN	3106-3	$4.95
ALL THE WAY	3023-7	$4.95
ALL-STUD	3104-7	$4.95
AMERICAN PRELUDE	170-5	$4.95
ANDREA AT THE CENTER	206-X	$4.95
ANGELA	76-9	$4.95
ANTHOLOGY OF CLASSIC ANONYMOUS EROTIC WRITING, AN	3140-3	$6.95
APPLICANT, THE	3038-5	$4.95
ARENA, THE	3083-0	$4.95
ASK ISADORA	61-0	$4.95
AUTOBIOGRAPHY OF A FLEA III	94-7	$4.95
B.M.O.C.	3077-6	$4.95
BAD HABITS	3068-7	$4.95
BADBOY EROTIC LIBRARY, VOL. 1, THE	190-X	$4.95
BADBOY FANTASIES	3049-0	$4.95
BAYOU BOY	3084-9	$4.95
BEAST OF BURDEN	3105-5	$6.95
BEST OF MARY LOVE, THE	3099-7	$4.95
BIG SHOTS	3112-8	$4.95
BIZARRE DREAMS	187-X	$4.95
BONE	177-2	$4.95
BOUDOIR, THE	85-8	$4.95
CANDY LIPS	182-9	$4.95
CANNIBAL FLOWER	72-6	$4.95
CAPTIVE MAIDENS	3014-8	$4.95
CARNAL DAYS OF HELEN SEFERIS, THE	3086-5	$4.95
CAROLINE'S CONTRACT	3122-5	$4.95
CAROUSEL	3051-2	$4.95
CATALYST, THE	3015-6	$4.95
CHAINS	3158-6	$4.95
CHARLEY'S GAME	221-3	$4.95
CHINESE JUSTICE & OTHER STORIES	3154-3	$4.95
CINDERELLA	3024-5	$4.95
CITADEL, THE	198-5	$4.95
CLAIRE'S GIRLS	3108-X	$4.95
CLARA	80-7	$4.95
COMPLETE EROTIC READER , THE	3063-6	$4.95
COMPLETE PLAYGIRL FANTASIES, THE	3075-X	$4.95
CRUMBLING FAÇADE	3043-1	$4.95
DANCE HALL GIRLS	44-0	$4.95
DANGEROUS LESSONS	32-7	$4.95
DARLING • INNOCENCE	3047-4	$4.95
DEADLY LIES	3076-8	$4.95
DELICIOUSDAUGHTER, THE	3155-1	$4.95
DEMON HEAT	79-3	$4.95
DEPRAVED ANGELS	92-0	$4.95
DEVA-DASI	29-7	$4.95
DISCIPLINE OF ODETTE, THE	3033-4	$4.95
DISTANT LOVE	3056-3	$4.95
DOCTOR IS IN, THE	195-0	$4.95
DREAM CRUISE	3045-8	$4.95
DUKE COSIMO	3052-0	$4.95
ECSTASY ON FIRE	3080-6	$4.95
EIGHTH WONDER	200-0	$4.95
END OF INNOCENCE	77-7	$4.95
ENGLISH GOVERNESS, THE	43-2	$4.95
ENTER WITH TRUMPETS	197-7	$6.95
EQUINOX	3157-8	$6.95
EROTIC ADVENTURES OF HARRY TEMPLE, THE	3127-6	$4.95
EROTOMANIA	3128-4	$4.95
EVIL COMPANIONS	3067-9	$4.95
EXPOSED	3126-8	$4.95
FAUSTUS CONTRACT, THE	167-5	$4.95
FESTIVAL OF VENUS	37-8	$4.95
FIRST PERSON	179-9	$4.95
FORAPIRATE'SKISS	3156-X	$4.95
FOR SALE BY OWNER	3064-4	$4.95
FRAGRANT ABUSES	88-2	$4.95

THE MASQUERADE EROTIC LIBRARY

FURTHER ADVENTURES OF MADELEINE, THE	04-1	$4.95
GARDEN OF DELIGHT	3058-X	$4.95
GAY ADVENTURES OF CAPTAIN GOOSE, THE	169-1	$4.95
GLORIA'S INDISCRETION	3094-6	$4.95
GOLDEN YEARS	3069-5	$4.95
HAREM SONG	73-4	$4.95
HAVEN, THE	165-9	$4.95
HEAT WAVE	3159-4	$4.95
HEIR • THE KING, THE	3048-2	$4.95
HELEN AND DESIRE	3093-8	$4.95
HELOISE	3073-3	$4.95
HIGHWAYWOMAN, THE	174-8	$4.95
HITTING HOME AND OTHER STORIES	222-1	$4.95
ICE MAIDEN, THE	3001-6	$4.95
IF THE SHOE FITS	223-X	$4.95
ILLUSIONS	3074-1	$4.95
IMAGE OF THE BEAST, THE	166-7	$6.95
IMRE	3019-9	$4.95
INITIATION OF PB 500, THE	3141-1	$4.95
INITIATION RITES	3120-9	$4.95
INSTRUMENTS OF THE PASSION, THE	3010-5	$4.95
IN THE ALLEY	3144-6	$4.95
INTIMATE PLEASURES	38-6	$4.95
JADE EAST	60-2	$4.95
JAZZ AGE, THE	48-3	$4.95
JENNIFER	3107-1	$4.95
JENNIFER AGAIN	220-5	$4.95
JUDITH BOSTON	273-6	$4.95
KAMA HOURI	39-4	$4.95
KATE PERCIVAL	3072-5	$4.95
KATY'S AWAKENING	74-2	$4.95
KIDNAP	90-4	$4.95
KIM'S PASSION	162-4	$4.95
KISSOFLEATHER	3161-6	$4.95
KUNG FU NUNS	3031-8	$4.95
LADY F.	3102-0	$4.95
LAVENDER ROSE	208-6	$4.95
LEATHERWOMEN	3095-4	$4.95
LESSONS AND LOVERS	196-9	$4.95
LETHAL SILENCE	3125-X	$4.95
LEWD CONDUCT	3091-1	$4.95
LONG LEATHER CORD, THE	201-9	$4.95
LOVE AND SURRENDER	3082-2	$4.95
LOVE IN WARTIME	3044-X	$4.95
LOVE'S ILLUSION	3100-4	$4.95
LOVING DOMINANT, THE	218-3	$6.95
LUST	82-3	$4.95
LUST OF THE COSSACKS	41-6	$4.95
LUSTFUL TURK, THE	163-2	$4.95
LUSTY LESSONS	31-9	$4.95
MAN SWORD	188-8	$4.95
MAN WITH A MAID	3065-2	$4.95
MAN WITH A MAID II	3071-7	$4.95
MAN WITH A MAID: THE CONCLUSION	3013-X	$4.95
MANEATER	3103-9	$6.95
MANSEX	3160-8	$4.95
MARKETPLACE, THE	3096-2	$6.95
MASQUERADE READER, A	84-X	$4.95
MASTER OF TIMBERLAND	3059-8	$4.95
MASTERING MARY SUE	3005-9	$4.95
MAUDE CAMERON	3087-3	$4.95
MEMBER OF THE CLUB	3079-2	$4.95
MEN AT WORK	3027-X	$4.95
MIKE AND ME	3035-0	$4.95
MILES DIAMOND	3116-7	$4.95
MISS HIGH HEELS	3066-0	$4.95
MISTRESS MINE	3109-8	$4.95
MR. BENSON	3041-5	$4.95
MUSCLE BOUND	3028-8	$4.95
MY DARLING DOMINATRIX	3055-5	$4.95
MY LIFE AND LOVES (THE 'LOST' VOLUME)	52-1	$4.95

THE MASQUERADE EROTIC LIBRARY

NAUGHTIER AT NIGHT	3030-X	$4.95
NUNNERY TALES, THE	20-3	$4.95
OBSESSIONS	3012-1	$4.95
ODD WOMEN	3123-3	$4.95
ORF	3110-1	$6.95
PASSAGE & OTHER STORIES	3057-1	$4.95
PASSION IN RIO	54-8	$4.95
PAULA	3036-9	$4.95
PAULINE	3129-2	$4.95
PERSUASIONS	183-7	$4.95
PLEASURE THIEVES, THE	36-X	$4.95
PLEASURES & FOLLIES	26-2	$4.95
PRISONER, THE	3011-3	$4.95
PRIVATE LESSONS	3116-0	$4.95
PROFESSIONAL CHARMER	3003-2	$4.95
PROTESTS, PLEASURES & RAPTURES	204-3	$4.95
PROVINCETOWN SUMMER	3040-7	$4.95
RAWHIDE LUST	55-6	$4.95
RED DOG SALOON	68-8	$4.95
RELUCTANT CAPTIVE, THE	3022-9	$4.95
REPENTANCE OF LORRAINE, THE	3124-1	$6.95
REUNION IN FLORENCE	3070-9	$4.95
RITUALS	168-3	$4.95
ROMANCES OF BLANCHE LE MARE, THE	3101-2	$4.95
ROSEMARY LANE	3078-4	$4.95
RUN, LITTLE LEATHER BOY	3143-8	$4.95
SABINE	3046-6	$4.95
SACRED PASSIONS	21-1	$4.95
SCARLET PANSY, THE	189-6	$4.95
SCHOOL DAYS IN PARIS	205-1	$4.95
SCHOOL FOR SIN	89-0	$4.95
SCORPIUS EQUATION, THE	3119-5	$4.95
SCRAPBOOK	225-6	$4.95
SECRET DANGER	3111-X	$4.95
SECRET RECORD, THE	3039-3	$4.95
SECRETS OF THE CITY	03-3	$4.95
SENSATIONS	3081-4	$6.95
SEX ON DOCTORS ORDERS	3092-X	$4.95
SEXPERT, THE	3034-2	$4.95
SEX SHOW	225-6	$4.95
SEXUAL ADVENTURES OF SHERLOCK HOLMES, THE	3097-0	$4.95
SHADOWMAN	178-0	$4.95
SILK AND STEEL	3032-6	$4.95
SINS OF THE CITIES OF THE PLAIN	3016-4	$4.95
SISTER RADIANCE	215-9	$6.95
SKIRTS	3115-2	$4.95
SLAVE, THE	173-X	$6.95
SLAVE ISLAND	3006-7	$4.95
SLAVE PRINCE, THE	199-3	$4.95
SLAVES OF CAMEROON	3026-1	$4.95
SLAVES OF SHOANNA	164-0	$4.95
SLAVES OF THE EMPIRE	3054-7	$4.95
SLOW BURN	3042-3	$4.95
SORRY I ASKED	3090-3	$4.95
SPANISH HOLIDAY	185-3	$4.95
STASI SLUT	3050-4	$4.95
STOLEN MOMENTS	3098-9	$4.95
STORY OF MONIQUE, THE	42-4	$4.95
STUDENTS OF PASSION	22-X	$4.95
SUBMISSIONS	207-8	$6.95
SWEET DREAMS	3062-8	$4.95
SWEETEST FRUIT, THE	95-5	$4.95
SWITCH, THE	3061-X	$4.95
TABLEAUX VIVANTS	3121-7	$4.95
TALES FROM THE DARK LORD	3053-9	$4.95
TALES FROM THE DARK LORD II	176-4	$4.95
TELENY	3020-2	$4.95
THONGS	217-5	$4.95
THREE WOMEN	3025-3	$4.95
TITIAN BERESFORD READER, A	3114-4	$4.95
TOURNIQUET	3060-1	$4.95

THE MASQUERADE EROTIC LIBRARY

TURKISH DELIGHTS	40-8	$4.95
TUTORED IN LUST	78-5	$4.95
VELVET TONGUE, THE	3029-6	$4.95
VENUS IN FURS	3089-X	$6.95
VICE PARK PLACE	3008-3	$4.95
VICTORIAN ROMANCE, A	175-6	$4.95
WAYWARD	3004-0	$4.95
WEEKEND VISIT, A	272-8	$4.95
WET DREAMS	3142-X	$4.95
WET FOREVER, THE	3117-9	$6.95
WHITE THIGHS	3009-1	$4.95
WILD HEART	3007-5	$4.95
WOMEN AT WORK	3088-1	$4.95
YELLOW ROOM, THE	96-3	$4.95
YOUTHFUL DAYS	3018-0	$4.95
AGENCY, THE	216-7	$12.95
BEST OF *GAUNTLET*, THE	202-7	$12.95
BEST OF *SKIN TWO*, THE	130-6	$12.95
BIZARRE SEX & OTHER CRIMES OF PASSION	213-2	$12.95
DRIVING PASSION, A	134-9	$12.95
ELEMENTS OF AROUSAL, THE	230-2	$12.95
EROTIC COMEDIES, THE	136-5	$12.95
GOOD PARTS, THE	186-1	$12.95
HUSTLING: A GENTLEMAN'S GUIDE...	137-3	$12.95
MELTDOWN!	203-5	$12.95
MOTION OF LIGHT IN WATER, THE	133-0	$12.95
MY LIFE AS APORNOGRAPHER	135-7	$12.95
SALINE SOLUTION, THE	180-2	$12.95
SENSUOUS MAGIC	131-4	$12.95
STONED APOCALYPSE, THE	132-2	$12.95
SWEET TALKERS	192-6	$12.95
TEMPLE SLAVE	191-8	$12.95
UNNATURAL ACTS	181-0	$12.95
MAD MAN, THE—*hardcover edition*	193-4	$23.95

COMPLETE MASQUERADE CATALOG AVAILABLE UPON REQUEST.

FOR A FREE COPY OF THE COMPLETE MASQUERADE CATALOG, MAIL THIS COUPON TO:

MASQUERADE BOOKS
DEPT Y54K
801 SECOND AVENUE
NEW YORK, NY 10017
OR FAX TO 212 986-7355

NAME ____________________

ADDRESS ____________________ APT # ________

CITY ____________ STATE ____________ ZIP ____________

All transactions are strictly confidential and we never sell, give or trade any customer's name.